The New Order

ALSO BY KAREN E. BENDER

Refund
A Town of Empty Rooms
Like Normal People

The New Order

Stories

Karen E. Bender

Counterpoint
Berkeley, California

THE NEW ORDER

Library of Congress Cataloging-in-Publication Data
Names: Bender, Karen E.
Title: The new order : stories / Karen E. Bender.
Description: First hardcover edition. | Berkeley, California :
    Counterpoint, 2018.
Identifiers: LCCN 2018017448 | ISBN 9781640090996
Classification: LCC PS3552.E53849 A6 2018 | DDC
    813/.54—dc23
LC record available at https://lccn.loc.gov/2018017448

Jacket design by Nicole Caputo
Book design by Wah-Ming Chang

COUNTERPOINT
2560 Ninth Street, Suite 318
Berkeley, CA 94710
www.counterpointpress.com

Printed in the United States of America
Distributed by Publishers Group West

1 3 5 7 9 10 8 6 4 2

To Robert, Jonah, and Maia, with love

Contents

The New Order

Where to Hide
in a Synagogue

Everyone agreed on the name: the Advisory Board for Safety and Well-Being. The committee would be composed of me and Eva Silverman, and today we would walk through the synagogue, discussing strategies to help temple members in the event of an attack. Together, we would come up with a list of suggestions and write a preliminary report.

It was a clear day in early October, and though the air still held the faint heat of summer, I thought I could feel the underbreath of chill in the air. We lived in North Carolina;

Charlottesville was four hours away. I arrived at Beth-Em synagogue fifteen minutes early; I did not wait in front of the synagogue, for a reason I did not want to explain but that felt entirely right. I walked to the entrance of the sanctuary, but did not stay there long, and then I wandered into the parking lot. I have belonged to this synagogue for thirty-five years. My shoulders braced a little as the cars rushed past me, and I wondered, as they drove by, what the drivers were looking for, what they would see.

I waited for Eva to arrive. We had not seen each other in recent months. Thirty-five years ago, we met at the park, shortly after our family moved here from the Northeast. It was Sunday morning, which meant everyone in the town fled to church; the playground in the lush green park near our house was so empty, that first Sunday, I thought the whole town had fallen ill. My husband was away for work for the second weekend that month. The park was silent and the wet grass shone. As I helped my daughter, Adina, down the slide, I saw Eva walk up with her son, Jacob. I was so relieved to see another person. We gazed at each other, evaluating. It seemed, in that large, leafy park, we were the only people in the world.

"Hi," she said, her voice bright as aluminum; I examined her, trying to decide if she resembled my cousins or not. She sat on the bench beside me and glanced at the toys in my stroller. She spotted a plush blue star that said "Shalom" in Hebrew, a toy from a relative that I generally tried to hide. She smiled. "You're skipping church, honey," she said.

"Well, I believe you are, too," I said.

We have been friends for thirty-five years.

We were mothers together. We spent time in the playground watching Adina and Jacob, and we sat for many hours at her kitchen table. We discussed the shoddy curriculum of the temple Hebrew school, the lack of participation in the annual Purim carnival (except for a few members who did everything, like us). When she tried, for three years, to work toward a degree in nursing, I held up flash cards for her biology classes, and she attempted to answer them. She advised me to start my catering business, and she was my first client, bravely hosting a bridal shower for Cara Abrams so that I would have a job. We kept a biweekly date on the treadmill at the Y after my divorce, walking with great urgency toward nothing; it seemed, striding down that moving black mat, that we covered miles. We celebrated our fortieth, fiftieth, sixtieth birthdays together, ordering the crème brûlée at a nice French restaurant in Raleigh; we vowed to do so every decade as long as we could lift a spoon. And, a year ago, we stood together reciting the Kaddish for her husband.

I was the first person she informed, after her family members. His death was a shock to the entire congregation. I always admired the fact that she and Al had been married for forty-one years. After his death, I picked her up at her house each Friday night, Eva sitting, frozen, staring at the TV, and I drove her to services. I said the prayer for the dead for her when she stood up alone, those first weeks, when her grief was so unwieldy she was unable to form the words.

Now I saw Eva come around the corner. We hadn't spoken very much in the last year. After Al's death, she flew to Miami to stay with her son for a couple months, but when she returned, I called frequently to check in on her but she often did not return my calls.

I missed her and wondered how she was. I was eager to hear her suggestions for the Advisory Board for Safety and Well-Being, and I hoped that working together, we could reconnect.

My heart lifted when I saw her.

"Eva," I said. There she was, dressed as always in a Kim Rogers suit from Belk's. I reached out to hug her and she let me; there was the familiar softness of her shoulders.

"Hi, honey," she said. Her voice was both bright and hoarse; it sounded as if it were holding up a roof. "Good to see you! How are you?"

She always leaned on the word "you" so that it felt like an embrace. But now the you was just a you. It sat between us like a broken plate.

"I'm okay," I said, carefully. "But how are you?"

"I am—" she said. "I'm here."

"I've been—" I did not know what to say. "Thinking of you. Where have you been these days?"

I tried to hug her again, but she did not embrace me this time. All friendships have their own contract, and for over thirty years our friendship was built on the understanding that we could comfort each other. We were important to each other in this way.

"Harriett, honey, don't worry," she said. "I'm all right. One day at a time. Trying to stay busy. I may go on a cruise. Maybe to Jamaica—with Arlene Johnson, she likes them too."

"I don't know her," I said, trying to understand. I had never been on a cruise. "But that sounds very nice."

She nodded. "Peaceful," she said, softly. I felt an ache of sadness for her, for Al, for his absence. I didn't quite understand why she chose to go on a cruise, and, more to the point, I didn't know why she hadn't asked me. But I was glad to see her, and the board was waiting for our suggestions.

"All right then," she said. "Let's begin."

We walked into the entrance of the synagogue. The foyer contained three potted palm trees, a framed photo of the first rabbi from seventy years ago, and a glass case, about five feet tall, containing some candlesticks and mezuzahs from the gift shop. I had no background in security, but I tried to think of the space in an objective, technical way. Our first scenario, I thought, was to imagine what would happen if someone ran into the temple holding a gun.

I didn't have a gun, so I held up my ballpoint pen.

"I'm coming in," I said. "Go. Run."

Eva's face flinched; she stood there, confused.

"I'm standing here, shooting!" I said, sharply. "Go!"

Eva began to walk, with little quick steps, toward the exit. Her two-inch heels kept her from getting anywhere very fast.

"Too late," I said. "Bang. I've already shot you."

Eva stumbled slightly, and her left shoe fell off. She grasped a doorjamb and pushed her foot back into her shoe. We would all be dead, probably within seconds, if anyone entered the synagogue with a gun. This was obvious. This idea entered my mind as a fact, but felt remote, like someone else's thought.

"I don't know what to suggest," I said.

She finished squeezing the shoe onto her foot.

"Don't wear heels to services anymore," said Eva.

I didn't understand.

"In case you need to run," she said.

I wrote this down. We needed to add some clarification. No heels to services. Sneakers were now the recommended footwear for the synagogue. Or congregants could wear shoes they could discard in case they needed to move fast.

We walked into the sanctuary. It was an open room, with nothing to obstruct a shooter, except perhaps the brass chandelier imported from Eastern Europe, which was suspended from the center of the room. It was about two p.m., the hour the room contained the most light; I watched as the sun rushed through the stained-glass windows on the left side, pale red, yellow, and blue squares glowing on the maroon carpeted floor. There were twenty pews made of dark polished wood facing the bima. On the bima, the raised area in front of the synagogue, was the lectern where the rabbi stood and behind that, the large wooden doors of the ark. The sanctuary had been recently renovated, and the walls were the color of cream. I took a deep breath. The room was empty and the air was still as glass.

"So," I said, "where are the safest places to sit?"

We considered. The front row, on the right side, first two

rows, we thought, might be a reasonable choice if the attacker had a gun because it was possible (if you had no physical limitations) to reach the exit in nine steps. This was the number of steps that a child required; an adult could make it in fewer.

"So who gets these seats?" I asked Eva.

Should these seats go to the most elderly members, such as Ruth Mankowicz, ninety-two, who would, frankly, have to be lifted out because she would block traffic with her walker?

"The children," she suggested.

This was smart. No one could voice opposition to saving the children. But. Which ones?

"The children under age twelve, and the Youth Group behind them so that they can have help getting out?" I suggested.

But this would include Max Lowenstein, who was ten and feared by the Hebrew school teachers, for at about four p.m. the levels of his ADD medicine would start to dip. And Gina Gordon, who was twelve, and had mastered a general demeanor of caustic pity; I didn't know if she would help others or just bolt.

And then my thoughts turned toward the adults. Frieda Sonnenbaum, president of the Ladies Concordia Society, a successful real estate agent who wanted to be first in line for everything, so her velocity in reaching the exit would not be in doubt. But I wondered about her helpfulness, for she never called Eva when her husband was in the ICU. Mara Stein had, a few decades ago, told my teenage daughter she could not babysit her children anymore after Adina, among other things, started smoking and cursed loudly in front of the Sunday school a few times. And not even the worst words, in my opinion. Mara said Adina would not be a good role model for her children. I never forgot this. No seat for her.

I thought of the faces of various members of the congregation, which members I wanted to live and who I felt less committed to, and I did not want to make any of these decisions. "How can we recommend who will sit in these seats?" I asked Eva. She, too, seemed alarmed by this idea.

"I don't know," she said. "Maybe it's like the exit rows in an airplane? If you sit in these seats, and something happens, are you willing and able to perform these tasks?"

We looked at each other, considering.

"And if they say no?" I asked.

She folded her arms. "If they cannot promise to help, then they have to sit farther from the exit," she said.

We agreed that we were unable to recommend who should have the seats closest to the exit at services. As of now, we recommended that the temple policy for service seating should remain as it has always been: first come, first served.

Our footsteps made almost no sound as we walked across the sanctuary. I was aware of all the doors—two in the back, the side exit. Unease was spreading inside me, a dark, fluttery lake. I imagined how many steps a shooter would take, running in, and how many steps I would take, rushing toward Eva and pushing her to the floor. I knew I would protect her.

As I watched Eva walk around the room, I remembered all the time we had spent at her kitchen table. Many of those hours were spent studying with her; she tried to finish the pre-requisites to transfer to the university for a nursing degree. She wanted to be an OB nurse; this was her dream for many years. "Two more tests," I told her, "you can do it." At first she cried and told me she didn't know why she could never complete her courses, as she believed she would be an effective nurse; but when she sat down with the tests her mind just went blank. After a few attempts, she stopped trying. Her husband, Al, was a successful pediatrician. She said she wanted to be there for her children, Jacob and Anna; work would take her away from that.

I didn't believe her, but I pretended I did, as I could tell she wanted me to. It was the silent conspiracy of agreement that sometimes happened between friends. It was impossible, sometimes, to know what resided inside other people, even if you believed you knew them well. For three years, she tried to become a nurse, and then she never talked about it again.

I remember how she coached me on my business. She liked coming up with names: "A Thyme to Celebrate," or "Pepper and Spice," and suggesting what I should cook. She was the first to hire me, and I was grateful, and she was excellent at spreading the word. She had many ideas for advertising, and I understood that she wanted to be part of it, the way peo-ple often want to inhabit a friend's success. I found clients on my own, and I became known for my hors d'oeuvres and my cupcakes, and I remember when Eva asked me to cater a fund-raiser for a charity one Valentine's Day and I had to say no because I was already booked.

But I remember mostly when she sat with me when my

husband left. He had become very businesslike to me during that last year; he was remote because he now loved an executive assistant in Ohio. One night, he described to me what he thought our family was, an uninhabited sheet of ice; he described it in great, considered detail, this empty and glacial landscape. It sounded awful, and I did not recognize it, but it was true for him. When he was in Ohio, he said, the landscape was different, palm trees everywhere and he could feel the sun on his arms. This was puzzling because I knew there were no palm trees in Ohio. He told me this on a night when I was going to make dinner for him and Eva and Al. I was going to make brisket and then finish the pink cupcakes for the baby shower I was catering the next day.

I canceled the dinner. Eva still came over. I sat at the kitchen table and looked at the forty cupcakes I was supposed to decorate. My mind was a heavy, wet bag of sand. But Eva posed beside the cupcakes, the pink icing, and the silver candies to decorate them and said, "Do this." My hands iced the cupcakes and arranged the candies and she helped me carry them to the baby shower and through a stunning act of theater, I arranged the cupcakes on a tray, I passed them out to the guests, I assumed the persona of a caterer. I also assumed the persona of a mother. I fooled everyone. I was a person who got through one day and the next.

For a couple years after that, now alone, I wondered each morning as I woke up if today would be the day I dissolved. I did not know if I had been told that this was the proper response to great sorrow, or if my body would actually vanish in some way, though I was still, evidently, here. I did not know the form this dissolution would take, or if it would be sudden and violent, but each day I awoke, expecting it.

After some time this fear subsided, but I felt sure it had slipped somewhere else. Was it inside my body, my fingers, my arms? Was it in the back of the closet, in a cardboard box? And when it rose up, one day, what would it do to me? My daughter grew up; I loved other men; I was one of North Carolina's Women to Watch of 2001 and honored at a luncheon; I was on the board of the temple. But still, sometimes I woke up, and I waited.

We continued our survey of the synagogue. We wanted to be thorough and there were many sections to appraise. The left side of the bima was farther from the exit (the only other one being the wide doors we came through in the back) so the number of steps to that exit was about twelve, plus the route was blocked somewhat by the flower arrangement, which could be either hazardous or useful—it could cause a congregant to trip and be murdered or one person could hide behind a sizable arrangement. We could also encourage arrangements with thorns, as a measure of defense.

We walked through the center aisle, between the rows of pews.

The pews were benches constructed of cedar, with a back that was about four inches thick, and a seat, which was about two inches thick. I ran my hand along the tops of the pews, which were cool and solid, thick as doors; they seemed promising. They also had cushions on them, and Eva measured one with her hands—the cushions, filled with foam, were about two inches thick.

If you hid under a pew, you might be safe if there was nothing sticking out. Who might be able to do this? Deborah Manheim, a quiet girl who tended to press herself into a corner of the Hebrew school playground while the other kids played tag; she could maneuver herself under here. Or Chaya Weiss, the secretary for the Ladies Concordia Society for forty-seven years, who seemed to become a chair during the contentious meetings and emerged two hours later with several pages of meticulous notes; perhaps she could effectively hide under a pew. I tried to think of others who would not be noticed by a gunman, but who would reveal themselves through a too-loud gasp or tendency to sprawl.

But I imagined a guy running in, firing his gun at everyone around him, then simply bending over to look under the pew. There he might see Chaya Weiss lying very still, her hands over her eyes. It wouldn't matter how quiet she was. He'd kneel and point the gun at her head.

"This won't work," I said.

Eva paused. She held on to the edge of the pew.

"There's enough room," she said.

"How do you know?" I asked.

"Because I hid under it," she said. "A year ago."

Eva told me that, one afternoon, she slid under a pew. This was right after Al's accident. A Ford Explorer hit her husband as he crossed the street, and for a month, he was in the ICU; he never woke up. Eva told me this: she had been sitting in the synagogue praying for him when she felt suddenly exposed, the room filled with cold air. What she knew, with perfect clarity, was that she wanted to be under the pew.

Eva looked around the sanctuary, which was empty, and slowly arranged herself on her hands and knees. She lowered her head, slid under, and turned on her back so that she was staring at the bottom of the pew. The carpet flat against her back, surprisingly musty, a smell of earth coming off of it, she lay there thinking. It was not clear what she wanted, resting there. There was no peace to be found. She said she did not feel calmer, for there was no calm, not then nor when he died three weeks later, but she said there was a comfort knowing that no one could find her. No one would look under a pew, she said. No one would ask her how she was doing. Closing her eyes, she tried to press herself into each moment. She did not want, just then, to be a person, but under the pew, she felt, briefly, like something else.

"You didn't tell me you did this," I said.

"Honey," she said. "Why would I tell anyone I slid under that pew?"

I was, I'll admit, a little jealous she had come up with this, her own strategy to deal with fear.

"It's a good place to hide. You just keep your arms by your sides and legs together." She considered. "Maybe we can show them the best way to hide under a pew," she said. "I can bring them here and show them."

We walked across the bima and approached the ark. Now I regret that we did not take security concerns into account during our recent renovation. The ark, where we kept the Torah scrolls, had a large door concealing the closet that made up its interior. The doors were made of oak, and they were about two inches thick. Opening the doors of the ark, I stood back, examining what was inside; the three Torahs were arranged, a pale light glowing behind them. I was frustrated by the shallowness of the space, which I now thought could have been developed more strategically. Perhaps there was enough space here to store a gun or other weaponry. What kind of gun would be best? A handgun? A rifle? As I inspected the ark, I decided it could accommodate three members. However, the members would, unfortunately, have to throw the Torahs onto the floor.

"Three could hide here," I told Eva, "without the Torahs."

Eva looked at me.

"What?" she asked.

"They would grab the Torahs, toss them on the floor, climb in, and shut the ark," I said.

"Are you out of your mind?" she asked. "You can't throw the Torahs on the floor. What if the shooter stepped on them? I could see that happening. He might stomp on them on purpose. Or what if he shot them? What about that?"

There was something a little different about her posture, a little more resolute than I'd seen before, her shoulders set as though she was anticipating an invisible hand would reach across the room and shove her. This was her opinion. The Torahs could not be lying, unscrolled, on the bima while congregants huddled inside the ark.

"Eva, imagine people running for their lives. The ones who live can pick up the Torahs after. But there's more room for people if you toss them out—"

I put my arm inside the ark, measuring: two feet. The Torahs sat inside, quietly. Now I perceived each Torah as a torso. The Torahs took up the room of three people. I thought about who might fit in the ark—Tracy Sadler, Harry Witt, a couple ten-year-olds from the Hebrew school; they were small enough, but how long could they crouch in here? I imagined that they would get scared in the dark.

Eva leaned inside and examined it.

"No," she said. "They can squeeze in between them. We need to make a statement in support of the Torahs. To throw them on the floor is not what we stand for as a people. The Torahs are sacred. People will find a way to squish in."

I could not believe she was saying this. Perhaps she did not understand what was going on.

"Eva. Obviously, I understand the holiness of the Torahs. I do. But the Torahs are not people. They are scrolls," I said. "Do you hear what you're saying?"

"I'm saying we have to follow certain rules," she said. "I'm surprised you don't see that. I'm agreeing with you—people can climb into the ark if necessary. Beside the Torahs."

My heart began to march.

"You don't even listen when the rabbi reads from the Torah," I said. "I've seen you check your phone."

"I only did that once," she said.

"Come on," I said. "We can set out a policy. If there is an attack, congregants are permitted to remove the Torahs from the ark and climb in for safety purposes." I paused. "We can add, 'Congregants removing Torahs are responsible for getting them back into the ark after the shooter has left.'" I thought to add *if they are alive*, but I thought I'd leave that out.

"No, I will not support this," she said. "A bad precedent. I can't bear the idea of the Torahs on the floor. Others will agree."

I regarded Eva. She resembled herself, oddly cheerful and determined to finish this task. I blinked but there she was, her lips bright with the burgundy lipstick she always wore, the person I had known for many years. I was used to knowing her as a generous person. I remember when she helped me with those cupcakes, when she carried them to the bridal shower the next day. I was shocked that she was siding with the Torahs.

But then I remembered another time. I remembered the morning in July 2001 when she called me, excited to tell me how her son had finally, after a long search, found a job as a publicist in a marketing firm in the World Trade Center. And I remember, too, that morning in September, when she called to tell me she hadn't yet heard from him. Al was out of town. I went to her house to wait with her as she tried his number every minute, as though she could save Jacob with the speed of her dialing; she would hear the dial tone and punch in the number again. "Eva," I said, finally, "wait. He might be trying to get through." She stood up and stepped toward the sink and stumbled a little. I grabbed her arm so she wouldn't fall, and she looked at me, and her expression held a terrible, shocking heat; her fear was about to incinerate her.

Then the phone rang. And when she picked it up, her hand was trembling so severely, she had to pass the phone to me. I whispered hello into the receiver and waited and then I heard her son's voice. "Jacob, hello!" I said, and her eyes were bright with tears.

They talked for a few moments and Eva instructed him to stay in his apartment. Don't go anywhere, she told him, unless someone told him to leave, and then don't use the airports—call her and they would devise some other way. There was something firm in her voice I had never heard before. When she got off the phone, her face was set with a mysterious and absolute certainty. "It was my dialing, over and over, that saved him."

This was, of course, absurd.

"Eva," I said, carefully, "how was it the dialing?"

"I don't know. Trust me. It was."

I couldn't tell her she was wrong; I had no right to decide that. Though I knew that there was no real reason why he had been spared. But I noticed how she became very organized and deliberate after that moment. I thought, from time to time, about her expression, and how something changed in her that day. I remembered the fear in her eyes before she picked up the call, and then, when she learned her son was safe, the cool sharpness in her face—not calm but etched with a type of understanding. This same sharpness shaped her expression now.

She decided then how the world worked; this was what she thought.

I tried to speak in a more careful way, telling her, "No, the congregation will want to protect the people, not the scrolls of parchment—others *will* agree," leaning on the word "will" because it just seemed so obvious to me.

She laughed.

This was the one part of Eva I did not understand: the way she believed one idea, fiercely, and not another. And that was when I started having the bad feeling. I knew that, as members of this committee, we had to discuss these issues. But she was not interested in discussion. The Torahs, she said, had to remain in the ark, in their appointed spots. But the spaces between the Torahs, yes, they were certainly available to any congregants who could shove their way inside.

She nodded as though we had come up with a useful suggestion. I loved Eva; but now I had a sour, unhappy feeling inside myself. Perhaps we could return to this later.

We surveyed the back rows of the synagogue, which gave me a particular chilled feeling, for it was where my children, when they came to town, liked to sit, because my grandchildren, who were seven and five, often had to be taken outside when they became restless. But that was probably where the gunman would run in first, so it was likely that if my grandchildren (I was just thinking of this now) sat in the back, they might be among the first victims.

This idea made me stop for a second, and I set my clipboard down on a seat. I could not think anymore. I wanted to run out of the synagogue. I wanted to run out of this country (but to where?), I wanted to just keep running. But Eva was still on task.

"Could we set up rubber dolls toward the back?" Eva suggested.

"What?" I asked.

"You know, a few life-sized decoys so the shooter gets them first, uses up some bullets. It gives people time to run and duck—what do you think? Shouldn't we look into this?"

I made a note. I was having some trouble thinking this through. I had heard of companies that produced blow-up dolls, but not for this purpose. Perhaps this could be a long-term investment; life-sized rubber dolls to distract any shooters who rushed in. Though this would then present the need to build more seating in other parts of the synagogue, perhaps with carefully constructed wooden or steel sculptures to block bullets or shield congregants in vulnerable seating positions.

I was suddenly exhausted. My god! Aside from these problems, the temple needed a new roof. The refrigerator in the kitchen of the Social Hall was about to break. Attendance at services had been light of late; we were losing members. There was no budget for any of this.

"I think we've covered how to hide from a shooter," I said. "But that's just the first thing. Now we have to prepare for a bomb."

If someone threw a bomb into the synagogue, then there

were other considerations. In one scenario, the attacker could hurl a bomb through a window, which made seats by the stained-glass windows risky. Or he could burst into the room through the back doors and throw a bomb into the center of the room. In this case, sitting near the back was actually a safer choice, as the bomb would explode toward the middle or front of the synagogue, and maybe if Janet or Abe Rosen, who got here early to claim these seats with coats and purses, survived the force of the blast, and the fire, they might be able to run out the blown-out back doors. But what of Elena and Harry Blum, who liked sitting by the aisle and were terrified, paralyzed really, by loud noises, or Dawn Bloch, who had claimed the same seat in the center, the precise place a bomb might land, for forty-three years—what would happen to them?

My head was full of seating arrangements and blood and bodies and screaming people. I was starting to get a headache. I had to sit down.

"I know about bombs," said Eva.

"What do you mean, you know about bombs?"

"I do," she said. "I dream about them a lot." She told me about a recurring dream that began six months ago. In the dream, she was running toward a tall, brightly lit office building. It was located in a downtown part of a city, and stood amid a cluster of other office buildings, in a haze of streetlights and mist. She was running toward it, heading for a restaurant, to a dinner engagement for which she was late. As she approached the building, a bomb went off. She said she could feel the explosion inside her, a shock in her bones, as though the end of the world occurred far away and in the center of herself, and she watched the building collapse, like a sandcastle, releasing a cloud of dust, and then she turned and ran the other way, and she said she could feel the heat of the bomb behind her, along the backs of her arms, but it didn't harm her; she was never subsumed by it. In her dreams, she always lived, which I admired, as I thought it revealed some confidence within her. Sometimes she said she was a little closer when the bomb went off, sometimes charred cars would hurtle toward her, sometimes she would see bodies fly out of the building, but she would only watch this from a distance. Sometimes the heat was so fierce she thought she was dissolving, and then she woke up. She said she had this dream quite frequently since her husband's death. She believed that she knew quite a bit about bombs, though in real life, she did not.

From her dream, Eva came up with a strategy to deal with a bomb, which was this: jump out the window. The stained glass would, she felt, be shattered by a bomb, and so, in preparation, the temple should provide stepladders, with three steps each, beside the windows so that congregants could run up the stepladders and then jump out. The strategy for a bomb was not hiding, Eva believed, but running, and leaping out the window, and though she had a hip replacement several months ago she still felt confident she could, if necessary, jump out the window, because she had been able to jump successfully, from freeway overpasses and ledges of buildings, in her dreams. She remembered how good she felt, leaping to safety. Others could feel that way, too.

"Eva," I said, firmly, "jumping is not an option for many temple members."

She shook her head. "They can do it," she said. "We can have step stools available. We can have designated helpers." It was important to her that she could picture herself, and the others, carefully jumping out of the windows to the lawn below.

She must have noticed my skepticism, as she patted my arm. "We're going to have a decent list of suggestions for the board," she said. "Don't you think?"

I heard a hope in her voice that I understood. I watched her walk down the aisle, surveying the pews, the flower arrangement, the bima, and I was struck by the tentative nature of her walk. It was the walk of an old person, and I knew that now I also moved with the same care. How strange to be this person, in my late sixties. The shifts in our bodies, in this country, had all happened so quickly; our lives were long enough now to have arcs, rising and ending. Thirty years ago I sat with my husband, Tom, she sat with Al, the four of us, at a restaurant. Now it was just Eva and me left in this room. I wanted to return to the time when we were just ordering in a restaurant, when we were organizing the Purim carnival or deciding which dessert to split, before the end of love, before death, before we were assigned to write this report on how to stay alive in our own synagogue. I could not tell her how much I wanted to offer suggestions that would protect the congregants, how I wanted, too, to be able to run out the door.

Finally, we reached the front of the sanctuary. I had my final recommendation.

It was the easiest and most obvious: the use of armed security at the temple. I had found, with some research, that other synagogues around the country were using private security companies. They were hiring guards to stand in front of their synagogues during Shabbat services. Some congregations screened anyone coming into the synagogue, with guards searching purses; I had even heard of a temple that had an airport security gate, checking everyone who walked inside.

I had several questions regarding armed guards in front of the synagogue. "Eva," I said, "these are the points we need to figure out. Would this guard be in attendance at all services? Friday night and Saturday morning? During Hebrew school? Ladies Concordia Society meetings? The Men's Club? For what activities would we provide security for the congregants and which activities would we not? How would this guard be armed? Should we have more than one? How many?"

A guard was, in my opinion, essential for all Shabbat services, *at the minimum*, which would be paying someone (two people?) for a twenty-four-hour shift once a week.

I thought she would agree to hire a guard for both services and Hebrew school, but she said, "No. I don't think so. We do not need a guard."

I was shocked by the way she said this, her certainty.

"Why not?" I asked.

"How are we going to do this?" she said. "Place an ad? Interview people? How do we know they'll be good guards? How do we know they're not, well, Nazis themselves?"

It was one thing, in her opinion, to discuss not wearing

heels or hiding under a pew or jumping out of a window. It was one thing to create an imaginary escape plan. But it was another to hire a guard. "And when are they going to stand there? Just during services? We can't afford to have one around the clock. Plus, a guard present at all times may scare people. Or they may think there is illegal activity going on—"

"Eva," I said, speaking slowly, "I agree, it is not the most calming sight. But, please, think about the alternative. This makes the most sense—"

We were sitting in the sanctuary, close to where she had hidden under the pew, waiting to hear news about her husband. Outside, the afternoon sun remained bright, which seemed a peculiar deception.

"No. It's going too far," she said.

"What is going too far?" I asked.

"Honey, the real fear is ISIS. ISIS is going to come destroy us. What we need to do, really, is bomb ISIS. Not hire a guard."

A door was closing on my heart.

"Eva," I said. "Take this seriously. What are you talking about?"

"Don't you watch the news?"

"Which news?"

"The news I watch says the Nazi thing is overblown. ISIS is what to worry about—"

"Eva, didn't you see what happened in Virginia? They were carrying machine guns and yelling horrible things— didn't you hear this?"

She would not look at me. We sat in the sanctuary, in the pews, facing the bima. To others, it perhaps looked as though we were there for a simple and reasonable purpose. The light fell through the stained-glass windows onto the carpet. The squares of color lengthened, like roads, along the floor. I'll be honest; I had always been aware of the exits. But now I watched them with a new, sorrowful alertness. Our bodies made long gray shadows in the bright squares. Our shadows were ageless and identical. I stared at them, trying to figure out what they said about us.

She shook her head briskly.

"Nothing is going to happen," she said. She let out a small sound I could not identify; not quite a sigh. It tried to resemble relief.

"Why not?"

She called me when she was waiting to hear about her son. She called me after her husband died. Then, her voice was perfectly flat, like no human voice I had heard before.

"The son-in-law celebrates Shabbat," she said. "He would not allow this."

"Eva," I said, "that's crazy. Who cares if he celebrates Shabbat. For god's sake, people are arming themselves."

"Where did you hear this? I didn't hear—"

"Eva, please. Are you kidding?"

She did not look at me.

"Stop," she said, sharply. "Stop."

Her eyes were filled with tears.

"Eva, we're all scared," I said.

Once upon a time, Eva and I liked to sit together Friday nights. We sometimes shared the prayer book. We stood beside each other when the rabbi opened the ark. We were not young people. Sometimes I wondered who would, one day, say the Kaddish for us. Our voices sounded so similar when we murmured the prayers together. Now, as I sat beside her, I was afraid of anything she said.

The afternoon light fell, a deep gold, on the carpet. If we sat here long enough, the room would darken and our shadows would vanish. Now our shadows looked like monsters as they stretched, longer and longer, in the low light.

"Please, Eva," I said. "We need a guard."

She removed her glasses, took a Kleenex from her purse, wiped them off. She put them back on.

"We have our notes, honey," she said. "Look at our notes. We did our job. We have good suggestions—"

"It's not enough," I said. "It's not."

She blinked, her eyes brown and large. "Don't worry," she said. She patted my hand. Her hand was trembling.

Boom. There was a sound somewhere in the synagogue, a thudding sound. My heart jumped. I looked around; the banging was coming from the front door. Boom. Boom. Boom. Someone was knocking. It was three in the afternoon and no one else was in the building; the sound vibrated through the room. There was another knock, this time louder. The door shook.

Neither of us moved.

"Are they expecting a delivery?" asked Eva.

"I don't know."

"Is it the rabbi?"

"Wouldn't he have a key?"

There was a pause, and then the banging on the door continued. Eva and I sat beside each other in the empty room; she smoothed down her jacket, her fingernails painted a pale pink. She touched the ends of her gray bobbed hair. She moved very slowly, with a deliberate quality that I recognized. Her face held no expression, was blank as a cloud. I stood up halfway in my seat, gripping the front of the pew. We turned our bodies toward the door but did not step toward it. "Hello?" I called softly. "Hello?" A silence, for a moment, then two; we stood, watching. Perhaps it was no one. But then—the pounding began again. A couple sharp knocks, then faster. The door was trembling. I waited to begin to dissolve. What would vanish first, my skin, my arms, my hair? Eva grasped my forearm, and I felt her holding on to me, and I held on to her, and we stood there, we just stood in that empty room as the knocking at the door grew louder and louder.

The Elevator

She was riding the elevator to her first job, as an assistant at a music magazine; the world fell away as she rose to the fifteenth floor. She was twenty years old. During the few months she had worked in this office, she had learned how to move names from column A to column B for event invites, make a collated set of Xerox copies, carry a cardboard box full of six different coffee orders. There was something remarkable and sparkling about all of it, the fact that, each morning, she entered the waiting room and did not have to remain there like the others, but was allowed to walk through the doors into the crammed gray hallways. The glaring fluorescent lighting stretched across the ceiling, the glass-windowed offices surrounding the main area like individual aquariums—she loved all of it. Entering the offices was like walking into a stranger's enormous, beating heart. She went to work each morning hoping the editors might soon trust her with more interesting tasks, for she wanted to show them everything she was capable of, which was endless and vast; however, each day, they asked her, barely looking at her, to do the same dull things. But today she wanted to change the editors' view of what she could do. She was going to ask for more responsibility. She had practiced this, with her roommate, was thinking about how to set up an interview with the lead singer of the Go-Go's, if she should just call the musician's publicist or ask the editor first.

It was a slightly shabby elevator, in need of renovation, with the feel of a bathroom from the 1970s, the pink artificial marble-like panels faded, like almost invisible veins. The carpet was the color of a pale sky and always held the bitter odor of cleaning chemicals. The doors closed. She stood, examining the numbers flashing on the strip at the top of the elevator, and was only vaguely aware of a man standing in the elevator with her, and that they were alone.

The man turned to her and said, "I could rape you."

Her thoughts, curving in one direction, stopped. They looked at each other. He smiled, as though this were a joke. An iciness flashed through her. She was new to office buildings, and she didn't know—was this a joke men in offices made?

He was of indeterminate age, perhaps forty or fifty. The age at which some men developed a soft, vulnerable chin. His skin was a pinkish shade of pale, as though he never got out in the sun. The low lights in the elevator made him look glazed, made of ceramic.

She remembered how he looked at her then, rapt, as though this were a discussion they had been having.

She remembered wanting to ignore this statement and get back to her previous thoughts, but her thinking had been stopped by this. The man moved toward her and she stepped back, and he touched her shoulder in a gesture that appeared strangely paternal, except for the fact that his other hand reached over and squeezed her breast, just for a moment, holding it as though he wanted to test its presence. She felt her body gasp. She understood that, in that moment, anything could happen. The elevator doors opened. He darted out without looking back. The doors closed and she was alone in the elevator now, which slowly took her to the fifteenth floor.

So many years ago. It happened so quickly. Sometimes she wondered if she had imagined it. But why would she imagine someone saying anything like that? And since that time, when she found herself alone in an elevator with anyone, she got out. She got out even when she was with her children, when they were young, eight, ten, if it was just them and a man she did not know on the elevator. She noticed when people were getting off floors. A hot cloud rose in her, though she appeared calm; she would grab her children's hands and step out onto the wrong floor while the person inside stood, watching.

"This isn't our floor," one of the children would point out.

She pretended not to hear and then said, "Oh. Wait a sec."

Slowly looking around, waiting for the elevator door to close. Sometimes the man inside would try to be polite and hold the door for her, waiting for her to step back inside, which was not what she wanted.

"Don't wait, go ahead," she'd say, waving her hand.

She would wait for the doors to close.

She had ridden many elevators in her life. When she graduated from college, she rode one to the twenty-sixth floor of the publicity firm where she worked as an assistant. When she got married, she worked at a company on the sixteenth floor. When she had her first child, she was still at that company, with that terrible supervisor who promoted the coworker who sat on his lap when he asked her to; she remembered walking by the supervisor's office and seeing the woman perched on the edge of his leg, and occasionally she heard laughter that sounded like bullets were hitting the wall. Then she left that company and worked on the twenty-sixth floor of another building, a very fast, almost brutally efficient elevator, which never made any sound. It whisked her to the floor where many of the employees seemed to be sleeping even when they were perfectly awake. Somehow, this brought out a more authoritative part of herself, and she listened as she told people what to do, and often they followed her direction. Trying to wield this authoritative voice in other places—in the kitchen, in doctors' offices, in principals' offices—trying to press down the words slowly, to sound calm. The way the world came at you. The way hearts gave out, suddenly, the way children had their own plans. The feeling of always wanting to know what to say, to be prepared. That office, on the twenty-sixth floor, was in New York City, a very tall, dark granite building with a view of Broadway facing north from Thirty-Fourth Street, and the lights trailed out, bright necklaces, glittering strands that she wanted to grasp and climb like ropes. So she pulled herself along, year after year.

The company where she worked for the longest period, ten years, was located on the thirty-seventh floor. She had become the senior editor at a textbook company, overseeing history books for middle grades. She was proud of the way she shaped the textbooks. She could tell the students what about the past was important to remember. Sometimes she thought back on the moment when the man in the elevator had turned and looked at her. She thought about that deliberate, unexpected shaping of the day. What had he gained, for himself, with that action? When she had walked off that elevator, she had, in some automated version of herself, walked to the assigning editor to ask her how to interview the music star. She did not remember what the editor had answered.

She felt the city, the pounding of steel cranes, construction, the watery swish of cars, vanish as she rose to her places of employment, as she stood in the rising elevator, a sensation, in the soles of her feet, of both lightness and fear. The numbers flashed in elevators all over the nation, in Los Angeles, in San

Francisco, in Atlanta and Miami and Houston and New York, the elevators all somehow united in this cause, taking people up and up and up and up to some bruised version of usefulness, or simply the slow shuffle through each day, all of these elevators rising as people stood, eyes gazing at the numbers above the doors, the oddly human sound of inhaled breath as the elevator rushed through the chute, as the employees were lifted to the floors where they worked, to the seats that they claimed, to the windows they gazed through, as the sunlight hit the city, the buildings glinting in the radiance like columns on fire.

The memory of that moment in the elevator dissipated, buried under the tumult of her life, but it was maintained in her bones, in the structure of her posture, for when she stood in elevators, there was always this subdued alertness.

One day, when she was in her mid-forties, past the time when she was perceived as a young woman but not quite sliding toward being old, she was in the elevator, heading to a meeting. She was thinking about the fact that she had to check on a statistic about casualties in the Battle of Gettysburg. So she did not notice when the elevator had let out people on the thirtieth floor.

And then, on the thirty-first floor, the elevator lurched, as though it were a heart beating irregularly, and, with a perverse, cheerful whistle, stopped.

She put her hand on the elevator wall to steady herself. There was a sound like water rushing outside of the elevator, but there was no water anywhere. She waited.

The door did not open.

"What the hell," he said.

There was one other person in the elevator.

He was bent over, his hand rummaging through a briefcase. He was tall, taller than she was, perhaps six feet. She saw the flash of his arm, but not his face. She had not been aware of anyone here. How had she been so absent, just then? She had a meeting to attend, how could she not have been aware? The elevator was about eight by eight feet. She had never really perceived it as a space before. The gleaming bronze panels, the ads framed in glass. Prix fixe at Restaurant Villa Grande on Floor Twenty-Seven. The free six-month membership at the health club on the Concourse. The plea to come and explore Costa Rica. She wanted to step into these ads, out of here, out of the space now sealing her in.

She wanted to get out of the elevator. She pushed the door.

The thought crossed her mind that she could kill him. It was an impulse, an idea that rose up from her gut before she could understand it. She was startled by the sudden and savage logic of this thought, how it could rise up so quickly in relation to another person. How certain she was that he would try to attack her. The intensity of this thought embarrassed her, as she understood the tenderness that gave fruition to it, the way she cherished her own life.

She banged on the elevator door with her left fist and then

fumbled through her purse. All she had that approximated a weapon was a ballpoint pen. Her purse revealed some tawdry, ill-conceived faith in human nature. The elevator door made a deep, echoing thud as she hit it, and the doors remained shut.

"What the hell," she said.

She listened to her voice. Did it make her sound powerful? The concept itself seemed a joke.

She jabbed the Emergency button on the panel but it did nothing.

She did not want to look too closely at the person beside her. Perhaps if she kept staring at the lights on the elevator, he would stand, frozen, as well.

She banged on the door again.

The smell of orange gum and bacon. What was it? The odor of his breath. There was no place for breath to vanish here. He coughed.

She had not felt fear that first time—there had been no time to feel anything. Now it rushed up, a hot force, her heart turning over and over, her entire being wanting to get out of here, away, to pour through the solidity of these elevator walls. She wanted to hit the doors so hard they broke open. Her fear was embarrassing, and for this to be visible seemed shameful, would reveal her as crazy, and she was not. She was a deliberate, organized person. She had worked hard in her life and she was proud of the textbooks her company created, she was proud of what students learned from them; she had attended her children's dance performances and purchased school supplies and driven her family from one place to another. The heat charged through her throat, her arms, her face. She did not even know where it was rising from. She pretended to laugh—a hoarse sound, like a scrape—thinking perhaps that would defuse the situation, even though she knew nothing about the man standing in the elevator with her, could not describe the discussion they were having, silently, in this elevator, without looking at each other. But they were having this discussion, of course, standing here, staring at the elevator doors, which remained, solidly, shut.

Open, she thought, looking at the doors. *Open*.

She would walk out, whole, untouched; the doors would just open and she would walk out.

Sit down, she told him in her mind. Sit down. Like a child. Perhaps she could convince him. Go. Marry someone. Drive to Utah. Support public schools. Watch TV. Eat popcorn. Go outside and walk. Listen to me.

What was he saying to her in his mind? She didn't know. She listened to the wet sound of chewing.

There was a rustling and he moved and there was a sense of crystal breaking inside her chest as she darted back and he banged on the elevator door.

"Somebody!" he yelled. "Open up!"

From the back, he appeared young. Perhaps twenty, twenty-five. He was wearing a navy suit; it did not fit him well; the jacket stretched across his waist and was a little baggy in the shoulders.

"Jesus," he said.

He turned toward her. His expression was not threatening; nor was it comforting. She wanted to place him, quickly, but she could not. He was in a rush. He looked like he had shaved, with purpose, this morning; his face was pinkish, raw. He banged on the door again and the elevator walls shuddered.

"Come on!" he called.

He was probably over six feet tall, soft, almost feminine around the waist and hips. He glanced at her, for a moment, as though he were waiting, in a hopeful way, for her to protest his banging, but she wasn't going to get into that.

She stood, half on the balls of her feet. They felt light; fear had emptied them.

"Push the Emergency button," he said to her.

She looked at him. She didn't like the way he spoke to her. Push. The button was on the panel beside her. She had already pressed it.

"I did," she said, icily. She pushed the button again, and there was a high, wheezing sound, as though some essential circuit had broken. "Look."

She saw him step toward the button panel; she quickly stepped back. He leaned forward and pushed it, too.

"No," he said. "Dammit. No."

She felt protected, somehow, by her age, the idea that she was too old, too wilted now to attack; but perhaps she was just thinking this to comfort herself.

"They're fucking going to fire me," he said. He jabbed the Emergency button again.

He assumed she was listening. She pushed down the reflexive urge to comfort him, to say anything. He was not the man who had spoken to her those many years ago. But what had been left on her, the residue over all these years, was the idea that he could be.

This man in the elevator was anxious; she could see that, his glossy, dark hair a little damp around his forehead. His lips were red as if he had been eating a Popsicle, his features brisk, alert as though filled by a gust of wind in the back of his head.

He pushed the button one more time, and there was the long, hoarse shriek the button made.

"What a fucked-up building," he said. He staggered back and leaned against the wall. "Why are you so calm? Don't you want to get out of here?"

She couldn't help it; she almost laughed. She didn't answer.

"Don't you?"

She stared at him. She could say nothing. She put her palm on the elevator door in case she could feel a vibration, a prelude to the doors opening, when she could jump out.

He squinted at her, as though the elevator had gone dark. It was painfully bright, actually. There was a chandelier in this elevator; perhaps some perverse person had tried to imagine this metal chamber as a living room. She noticed, for the first time, that the chandelier was broken, two of the dangling crystals chipped. The light from the chandelier glared so strongly she could almost see the shadow of his skull in his face; she wondered if he could see hers as well.

He sighed, sharply.

"They're going to kill me," he said. "Do you hear me? They. Are. Going. To. Gut. Me."

That last sentence made her jump a little; she gripped the ballpoint pen in her purse.

He slid down so he was sitting on the dusty floor of the elevator and rubbed his hands over his face.

She watched him. She was taller than he was at this moment. She wondered if she heard sounds of life outside the elevator, or if she was imagining it, the rumble of footsteps, a door slamming, a woman's laugh. But it felt as though the world had vanished, leaving only this cramped elevator stall, the golden walls gleaming in the relentless bright light from the broken chandelier. She had never quite noticed the golden walls of the elevator, how their grandeur implied some innate failure about the people riding it, how the riders would see, out of the corners of their eyes, blurred, gold reflections of themselves.

The man was speaking into the palms of his hands. "They said be there at three p.m. on the dot with the photos or don't come in. Fuckers. I just know Smith planned this. I bet she's stopped the elevator right now."

She stood, silent.

He released a sharp sigh. "Smith! I see you! You cunning bitch. You can't do this! I'm watching you right now."

He spoke the words directly to the elevator doors. His anger toward Smith seemed like a form of longing. She felt he was waiting for her to ask a question about Smith. It was a hunger she could feel, palpably, in the elevator, and, as a mother, was familiar to her. His own mother had, it seemed, ignored him or belittled him. She stood, sensing that hunger all around her, and, with enormous effort, she did not answer it.

She was aware of her own hunger, huge, yawning inside her, to get out of here. She needed to get to her meeting. Today they would discuss ways to organize information about the end of the Civil War. The supplementary online material linked to chapters in the textbook, what was the budget and who they would hire to write it? The regular plans, how luxurious they now seemed. The staff was probably talking about her now, wondering where she was. She was ridiculously punctual, never absent or even late. But she was not afraid in the same way he was; well, she was, a little, but she was one of the senior people in the company, which protected her from the consequences of being late. The broken elevator was, after all, not her fault. They would, she assumed, be worried, but someone from maintenance would apologize, she thought. Are you all right? They would ask. I hate getting stuck in elevators. They would think it an inconvenience. They would not think of the others in the elevator with her, the travelers in this small, close space lifting eyes to their particular destination.

He was afraid, for other reasons, and she sensed his fear, thick in the air. She felt relieved, and fortunate: her fellow employees would, she believed, not punish her for her absence. She was, she thought, not in the same situation that he was in, and understood that she could not reveal this to him.

"She planned this," said the man, his voice a little hoarse. "You know? I could see it when she was sitting at her desk just staring into space and pretending to do nothing, but she was. I know it. Thinking about me."

She watched him gaze at the elevator doors, staring at whoever was on the other side. What was this Smith doing right now? She imagined a woman in a trim black suit walking quickly down a hallway, holding her coffee carefully away from her. Did this Smith, whoever she was, think of him, or notice him, or even know who he was? She remembered all the times she had thought of the first man in the elevator, and how she wanted to erase him from her mind, and wondered if perhaps that was part of what he had intended, to remain in her mind in that way, to establish this, a presence.

Her heart was still marching, full, and she was alert. He was still sitting on the floor, his long legs stretched in front of him.

The space held a peculiar, motionless heat, a dead, quiet airlessness. The elevator hung over a long, dark chute, nineteen floors above the ground. It did not move, but she was aware that they were standing in a fragile metal box, glancing at their golden selves as the elevator was suspended in the stale air.

He glanced up at her. "Why don't you say anything?" he asked.

She was not going to answer. She was going to stand there; her palm made a pale imprint on the gleaming elevator doors.

He regarded her, his eyebrows lifted. He was, she thought, trying to figure something out. Perhaps he thought she was deaf. Should she pretend she was deaf? Maybe she should pretend she had a disease. Didn't people do that, sometimes, to dissuade others from approaching them? On the elevator door, her hand was just barely trembling.

She could sense him wanting her to speak, so that he would not be alone in this elevator. She understood, though she did not share this—he did not want to be alone. It had only been a few minutes, but it seemed the rest of the world had become nothing. Its presence was quiet and unknown. But she liked not speaking. He knew nothing about her. What was he guessing? Whom did she resemble? Did she think she was his mother, his sister, his girlfriend, what? Her own life felt like an exercise in deception. There was the meeting she was about to lead, the glorious and unsettling moment when the staff, assembled around the table, clutching Styrofoam cups of coffee, eyeing the rubbery muffins on a paper plate, waited to hear what she had to say. The theater of the meeting itself, the fact that some people were assigned lesser positions, paid less money, even if they were smarter, or even better at their jobs, the heavy and living silence about this inequality, the fact that they all sat around the conference room, nibbling at the crackers or grapes, pretending that no one was aware of this. The fact that she sat at the head of the table, now, and that she was the one to call a meeting to order, that she tried to turn the direction of the company the way she wanted, that the other employees asked her for direction, even if they perhaps resented what she said. She was the first woman at her company to hold that position and found the view from her place at the table like gazing across a long, troubled sea.

The man sitting on the floor was looking at her.

"I've seen you," he said.

"What?" she asked.

"I've seen you with her. In the hallways. Yep. Sixteenth floor."

He examined her with a new shrewdness, a desire to figure something out.

"I don't work on the sixteenth floor," she said.

"Yes, you do," he said, sitting up. "You know her. Tell her I'm coming. I'm going to be at work. Tell her not to worry. I'm late because I had to buy the car. It's not my fault. Sheila said buy the car. I didn't want the car, I didn't want more payments, for fuck's sake, student loans. She wanted to ride in it. So I bought it. I'm not going to be late. Tell her. Come on. You're best friends, right? Tell her."

He was sitting straight up against the elevator, his face wounded with misunderstanding.

"See, I know," he said. "She probably texted you a few minutes ago to ask, is he in there, is he in the elevator and you said yes, in fact he is—"

"I don't know who you're talking about," she said, slowly. "And you're wrong. I don't work here."

She listened to herself speak.

"I'm never here," she said. "I'm never in this building."

Her body became still as she said this, for this statement, though false, described something she understood. She sometimes believed that she was not in fact in this building or this elevator or even in this precise body or life. Her actual arms and chest and legs felt almost weightless as she said this, adjusting to this new reality.

"I've seen you," he said, trying to look her in the eye.

"It wasn't me," she said, her voice louder as she went on, "it was someone else. I'm security. They called me. I'm here—I'm here to make an arrest."

He blinked, uncertainty unfurling across his face. She was right about something. He had done something he felt guilty about, whether it was criminal or not. He looked away; everyone is pierced by a form of guilt.

She wondered where the original man on the elevator was now, after thirty years; perhaps he was in a nursing home. Perhaps he was dead. She imagined him buried, a lawn stretched, a green haze, over him.

"There was a disturbance. Seventeenth floor," she said.

He rubbed his palms slowly along his thighs, as though trying to warm his hands.

"I didn't hear anything," he said.

"Half an hour ago," she said. "You didn't hear it. You weren't here. Well, we got a call. There was screaming. The secretary called us. There was screaming."

This was exactly what had happened. A part of her felt certain of this, even though none of it was true. This new reality presented itself to her as a clear relief. Her face was hot, but she hoped he could not detect anything true about her in the crushingly bright light of the elevator.

"Don't you hear them?" she asked.

"What the hell are you talking about?"

She laughed, and, that time, it sounded like a human laugh.

"I hear them," she said.

Standing by the elevator, she pressed her cheek to the golden doors. There were sounds, perhaps; running, the precise heaviness of masculine footsteps, the whine of a vacuum. Or nothing.

"Bullshit. Who do you hear? Who?"

She was not going to answer him.

"Sloan, it was Sloan I bet," he said. "Idiot was under so much stress. I saw him here yesterday, he looked like he was going to have a heart attack. Was it Sloan?" He tapped his fingers against the floor, almost joyful. They made a sound like mice running. He paused.

She held still, not saying.

"No it wasn't," he said. He stood up. "It was my girlfriend, she screamed this morning before she got out of bed, I made her scream, I'll tell you—"

He was standing beside her. His voice was heavy, as if a boulder were sitting on a piece of paper. His eyelid twitched.

"Not a scream like that," she said. "No."

He was silent.

"What? Was someone killing someone?"

Her cheek twitched; then she forced herself to look up, into his eyes. They were brown. She had expected them somehow to resemble a lizard's, but actually they looked more like a cat's, or, actually, like neither. She said, quickly, "There was an attempt. There was a lot of blood. There will be many arrests."

Her voice came out louder and flatter than she expected. He lurched back. There were surprising dark shadows blooming under his armpits. He banged on the door another time, and the door thunked so loud she could feel it in her face.

"That's not fucking true," he said, looking at her. "That's not—"

"It's true," she said. "You don't know anything."

"What the hell do you mean?"

"I know everything," she said, softly.

"You do? So what are they going to do now? In fifteen minutes?"

She heard something else, the thinness of his voice, as though he had been shouting forever. It seemed as thin as silk.

"They're on their way," she said, firmly. She had no idea, but felt certain she was right. It was, perhaps, what they both wanted to hear. She liked saying it. "They're on their way. I hear them."

She pressed her body against the cold elevator door. She listened, and there were no distinguishable sounds on the other side, nothing that told her anything about life out there, or whether anyone was coming to open the elevator, or working in their respective offices, or was present in the world at all; but there it was, she thought, the sound, a low roar, the almost imperceptible gargantuan power of the machinery of this building, the faint whirr, if not of screaming, of relentless hunger, of something else. The man in the elevator also pushed his shoulder against the door. He was facing her. He was perhaps two feet away. His cheek was pressed, with all of his weight, against the golden door, and his eyes were closed as he tried to listen to the screaming she claimed was on the other side. The broken chandelier above them flickered; it looked like it was about to go out. She was cold. The elevator doors were cold. She imagined, with envy, the day happening outside this building, the sun moving with its heat and brightness through the sky, and the shadows of clouds falling across the buildings, the sky blossoming from blue to yellow to orange to red to a darkness that revealed stars. She was not here, not in this place, not in any enclosure; she was here, with this strange package of herself, wanted to be out there, out there; she wanted to be everywhere in the world; she did not know how to get there. The smell of the man's orange gum was sickeningly sweet. She watched the man, her fingertips touching the door, waiting for a trembling, a vibration, waiting for sounds to indicate that someone was coming to open the doors and let them out.

Three Interviews

Finally, Ms. Gold was called in for job interviews—three of them. There had been silence for about seven weeks, this round, and then representatives from the Human Resources departments called all at once. She said yes immediately to each interview. She was delighted. Yes. Yes. Yes. Each job a reduction in salary and benefits from her previous position. The interviews were all scheduled for one day, and this last week she tried to find a new outfit to wear to them—the shirt or jacket that would convince the employers: Yes. Yes. Yes. Her. She stepped into stores that catered to the young, stores that sold to women twenty years younger than her. She tried to find outfits that would be appropriate for someone her age—she was on the other side of forty-eight—and stood in front of a mirror wearing a navy jacket with red rhinestone buttons on the cuffs. She liked the jacket, but she wasn't sure about the buttons. She turned around in front of the young salesgirl, who stood wreathed in a brilliant, kind smile, almost motherly, for which she must have been hired.

"What do you think about this for a job interview?" Ms. Gold asked, touching the rhinestones.

"You look terrific!"

The girl's voice was too eager to be sincere. Now Ms. Gold would have to ask the next question.

"I mean," she said, "is it all right for my age?"

The girl's eyebrows twitched, just slightly.

"Maybe," said Ms. Gold, reassuringly, for the salesgirl seemed to need rescuing from this question, from her.

She had been out of work for seventeen months. Before that, she had been, for many years, a senior reporter for a travel industry weekly; then the magazine fired half its staff. Since she walked out of the building, she was in this inchoate state: searching for work. She thought she had learned to calibrate her hope, that wild, muscular dog inside her—she learned to press it down. She thought sometimes that the dog might leap out of her, leave her empty, a husk. Or she tried to learn the precise balance between hope and a clear understanding of her prospects. She was not young. Or that was how others viewed her. She felt young, thirty-five maybe? An age when life still seemed to be an endless road. She wanted to undo whatever had gone wrong to get her to this place, the constant staring at the Internet job boards, the tense smiles when people asked her what she was doing now. The corrosive, luxurious domain of other people's pity. The employed people's pity. How much force it took to block that, a poisonous wind; all she needed was an office, a duty, a check. She knew she was a skilled reporter, she knew that. But to reach back and pluck out, like a gray hair, the flaw or action or incident that had led to this situation. And forty-eight, over a year without a job.

If she purchased this jacket, would the world open up for her or would it shut her out? The beauty and anxiety of each action was that it could lead to everything or nothing. She had not been in love in five years. It was no one's fault. The world doled out moments of light and then, when it wanted to, withdrew them.

All over the country, editorial offices were firing their staff. She imagined all of the reporters, proofreaders, copy editors lining up for interviews, out the door of the office, onto the street, there were swarms of them, and she wanted to brush them all away with a broom. Scattering them, like a thousand ants, out of her way.

Sometimes she sensed herself marching with all of the other unemployed people, all of them walking through the city with their résumés. It was a bond, though none of them knew it.

It was, sometimes, a loss to sleep alone, to miss the soft

breath of another beside her, to try to stay awake to avoid being parted by sleep; it was, at other times, a calm relief. But there was nothing good about this state, this frail ghostliness, without an office, a duty, a check; without the prescribed arc of her day, without the certainty of her salary appearing every two weeks in her checking account. She had not realized how seeing that money deposited each month was as vital as breath. She was grateful for the unemployment checks, but the shortfall felt physical, as though she had lost an arm or leg.

Today she climbed out of the subway with purpose; three chances, three jobs. Three places to go.

She had a two p.m. appointment at Elite Furniture Newsletters. It involved writing short pieces about the lamp industry. The company was in a building on East Thirty-Eighth Street. The office was located on a floor with a math-tutoring center, an online vendor of organic paints, and a wholesale mattress supplier. Three of the businesses on the floor were named Elite. Ms. Gold stood in front of the door to the office, and then she knocked.

Mr. Rana looked up as she walked in. His fifth that day, out of fifteen. He had allotted twenty minutes for each. The résumés were barely distinguishable. He was tired of them all. Truly, what he was thinking was: he did not know what to order when he met June for lunch at 11:30. He told her the lunch meeting was to go over the year's budget, but this was not true. He had worked here for one year. He was in Human

Resources, was the first line of elimination for the applicants, but, honestly, he disliked talking to people. His skills were in organization, telling people what to do, guiding them through forms, running the background checks. But he didn't like to talk to anyone, really, that was his secret—he was new to this country, and he tried to speak slowly, to help people with his accent, as people sometimes leaned forward, asking him to speak his sentences two, three more times until they understood. The register workers at Starbucks asking him to repeat his coffee order again and again. They were not intelligent people, he thought, not flexible; they could only hear one version of events in their ears. But when he talked to June, she always heard what he said.

She worked two floors below, in health-care benefits. She was very chatty, and she spoke quickly, lightly, freeing him mostly from the effort of speaking. He did not like to look directly into people's eyes, he was a little shy that way, but she did so in a way that was measured and calm. She was from Ohio. Toledo, she said. She knew the minutiae of details about dental plans and mental health coverage in a way that was actually breathtaking, that made her seem she had access to every detail in the world. She was smarter than most of the idiots who worked here; when he asked her for information, he received it. The way she looked at him when he spoke, with green eyes a shade he had never before seen, and that took him in but didn't invade, made him feel the moment he inhabited was sealed into itself, separate from a past and future.

But now he was distracted. He had wanted to talk to June

alone for a few months, and here was the opportunity. He didn't know what to order for lunch; he did not know what to say to June. What did she like to eat? He knew so little about her except the way her laugh made him feel.

The moment before the applicant walked in, he was thinking of June so intently, it almost felt as though the room in front of him didn't exist. He resented his cousin for getting him the job here—he had a good title, associate director, Human Resources, but his supervisors were young, former fraternity boys who barked orders at him in a way that made his skin a little cold. The furniture that he stared at ten hours a day, the office chair and bookcases, were so drab and leaden it seemed they were going to sink into the ground.

But here stood Ms. Gold, walking into this room with an enormous smile. All the applicants showed brilliant white teeth, as though they were about to eat him. She held out her hand.

"Yes," he said, shaking it. "Thank you for coming in."

She sat down. He crisply removed her résumé from the pile.

"So," he said, "tell me about your experience."

She leaned forward and launched in. She had that smooth recital of her past jobs, which had been honed by repetition. "I was at Fairchild for seven years, reporting and editing, then I was at *Travel Weekly*, as a senior reporter, then that magazine shut down, do you remember that? No warning, just here and then gone—"

She was trying to be casual, almost chummy, the false intimacy of Americans, which he found sad.

"What are your strengths and weaknesses?" he asked.

"I've never missed a deadline," she said, sitting up. "The idea doesn't even cross my mind. I am a quick learner. I'm a team player. Weaknesses? Sometimes I work too hard."

It was what everyone said—all of them, with serious expressions, claimed they worked too hard. Ha, when they saw how hard they would work in this position. How they all would gain weight hunched over their desks until nine at night. The job was a program to get fatter. He gently touched the fold above his waist, which had expanded since he had moved to the States. Would June hug, as he noticed her hugging some employees, or shake hands? He hoped she would touch his shoulders, not his waist. Though he also wanted her to touch his waist.

"I'm new to this but have so much enthusiasm," she said.

He felt sorry for this applicant, suddenly, for himself, stuck listening to her. She was American; she did not have to worry about visas, and though he had his green card, and though his country was not on the banned countries list, his cousins here on student visas were emailing every day, deciding if they should fly home in the summer or not. What would come next? No one knew what the future held. Ms. Gold, born in New Jersey, was safe. Her ease was galling. The distance between him and the person sitting in front of him felt like a hundred miles, farther away even than his family, thousands of miles away.

"I can see opportunities for articles about furniture in not just residences but hotels, restaurants—"

A restaurant. He forgot his next question. He tried to be casual, leaned on his folded arms. "Tell me," he said, carefully.

"What would you order at a restaurant when you are discussing a budget with someone? What dish?"

She studied him. He realized that she thought this was a real interview question.

"What type of restaurant?"

"Italian." June had mentioned spaghetti once; perhaps she liked Italian. "Maybe Casa Nonna. On Thirty-Eighth."

She rubbed her arms. "A budget. Lots of details. You don't want to be thinking about what you're eating. Perhaps not pasta then. Hard to eat noodles and be neat."

He nodded.

"Ravioli. Or a chicken cutlet," she said.

He would ask for a corner table, perhaps one away from the others. He imagined himself and June in a quiet corner of the restaurant, looking at one another. The image was so perfect he felt his arms burn. The next question simply rushed out; he could not stop himself from asking it.

"And if I touch her hand when I spoon food onto her plate? What then?" he asked.

He felt shame in his throat and wanted to grab the words back. Why would he even say this? He was not concerned about this. Yet he looked to Ms. Gold for her response. Her eyelid pulsed, as though she disapproved of what he had said. She sat forward. "Don't spoon food onto her plate," she said. "She can do it herself."

He had asked the wrong thing; this applicant thought he was infantilizing June, but really all he wanted was to be close to her.

"Yes," he said, as though this was obvious. "Thank you."

He noticed her résumé sitting flat on the desk.

"Tell me what you can bring to our organization," he asked.

She continued to describe her attributes, and he pretended to listen, but now he was embarrassed by the question he had asked. He wanted to be with June in that other room, not here; the other room, with its luster of assumed feeling. But what if June was not drawn to him? What if she only wanted an American, someone who had lived here for many years? How would she view him now? Where would he be then, but this shabby room?

He shook Ms. Gold's hand and told her they would call her in a week if they needed more information.

When she walked out the door, he envied this: that she did not work here, that she was heading on to another life. He felt the closeness of the room, the stale air inside of it. His face grew hot as he remembered what he had asked her. How had that happened? What would she think of him for asking this? Embarrassed, he slipped her résumé under the stack and thought again about what he should order for lunch.

Ms. Gold walked onto the bright street. She thought she performed well during the interview. But then he had asked that strange question about the restaurant, and the hands. What was he trying to learn from that question?

What would happen if he touched her hand? It was not a

question she prepared for, really. How could that relate to writing pieces about furniture? Did he actually want to ask *her* to lunch, and was this his awkward way of doing so? What did *that* say about this office? She thought of the last time she had touched hands with someone, deliberately, to feel their softness against hers, that brief promise, which made her hand feel fragile against another, unreal. It was several months ago, a fact that she did not want to admit. The clouds fled across the blue sky. Around her, people rushed by, clad in uniforms that proved they were useful. There was the businessman, there was the falafel vendor, there was the messenger, there was the security guard.

The second interview was at a small media company devoted to bimonthly magazines on yoga, herbal medicine, and trends in massage therapy. The air in the waiting room smelled aggressively of lavender. She wanted this, an associate editor position organizing content on new trends in yoga wear. For this job, she believed she should look younger. She went into the restroom and rubbed more foundation into her face. Did the restaurant question at the last interview mean that she looked younger than she was? Did the brushing the hand question mean that he wanted to brush hers? She touched the back of her own hand with her fingertips, trying to detect her future.

Mrs. Barron stood up quickly when Ms. Gold came in and grasped her outstretched hand as though reaching for an animal about to vanish into a hole; firmly, she shook it. "Good to meet you," she said, sharply, and then sat down.

Mrs. Barron settled behind her desk like it was a barricade. Mrs. Barron was a tall woman with blonde hair who looked like she had been dropped into her suit from a great height; her jacket flowed around her like water. She watched Ms. Gold sit in the chair in front of her desk.

"I've reported on numerous topics, but I just started taking yoga myself," said Ms. Gold, speaking quickly. "And I want to know everything about it."

What Mrs. Barron noticed, immediately, with a swerve of pain, was Ms. Gold's hair. It was the same haircut as her daughter's. Short, parted on the side, dark red.

Mrs. Barron looked down at the résumé so as not to stare at the applicant. Her daughter, Beth, had left home thirteen months before and had not called her since. She was just eighteen years old. Her only child. Beth had called others— her father, who lived in Michigan, her cousins, who lived in Connecticut—to share with them the details of her new life. She had moved to a small town outside of New Orleans. Why Louisiana? What could she want there? Her mother wanted crisp, factual information. A job. Love. New scenery. Cajun food. Mrs. Barron bribed one of the cousins for the cell number. She called it, or sometimes texted.

How are you?

There was no response.

Why?

She wanted to reach forward and brush the applicant's hair.

"Tell me about your experience," said Mrs. Barron. "It looks excellent."

She could see how the word "excellent" stuck in the applicant's mind; she wished she hadn't said it. Mrs. Barron didn't know why she felt the need to flatter her—but she remembered what her daughter said to her before she left: *Stop criticizing me.* She thought she had said so little. *The school will send you home if you wear a crop top. Don't go to Jordan Spangler's apartment, I heard she uses drugs. You failed the history test because you didn't study.* The girl looked so frail to her, so small—wasn't it her job to protect her? But the girl always heard something sharp in her voice, something she wanted to escape.

"Thank you," said the applicant. "I have read *Yoga Focus* with much interest over the years. It's the only place I go for coverage of yoga. You learn about all the positions—pardon the pun—all the angles I want to know about."

No, thought Mrs. Barron, *no yoga jokes.* "How do you see yourself in our organization?"

"I am excited about the opportunity to be associate editor," said Ms. Gold. "I've been that before, as you can see, but am more than happy to do it again. I can write for print or digital, you can see my social media platform—"

Mrs. Barron last saw her daughter, just over a year ago, when Beth was about to start a job as a counselor at a YMCA summer camp. She had thought Beth was going to spend the night at a friend's house. She remembered how her daughter quickly packed an overnight bag, grabbed some granola bars from the kitchen, and a loaf of sliced bread, which seemed odd, and put them in her backpack. Then she stopped at the door and looked at her mother.

Beth knelt and rummaged through her backpack.

"What are you looking for?" her mother asked.

"A hairbrush."

Mrs. Barron then headed into the bathroom to get her a hairbrush. But when she came out, her daughter was gone.

She stood in the empty apartment, clutching the hairbrush, an alarm sprung in her chest, and she understood what she would feel in the next few days and weeks and months, the unbearable rush to claim nothing, the approaching tidal wave of pain, and she ran out the door into the hallway to give her daughter the hairbrush, as though this was the object that would solve the tension between them. But Beth, in some new resourcefulness, had willed herself to vanish.

Mrs. Barron carried the hairbrush with her everywhere since her daughter vanished. She sometimes reached into her purse and touched the handle, to make sure it was still there.

Now she looked at the applicant, who was sitting perfectly still, hands clasped, but gave the impression that she was in a slow and constant state of motion.

"May I ask you to do something?" Mrs. Barron asked.

The applicant leaned forward slightly.

"It may sound odd but—" Mrs. Barron laughed, and the applicant's face became very still, alert. "It's part of the interview. A test we do. I'll explain later. You need to, well, pick up your purse."

Ms. Gold's cheek twitched. She picked up her purse.

"Now look through it."

She unzipped her purse and began to dig through its contents.

"Now ask, I need a hairbrush."

Ms. Gold glanced up. "I need a hairbrush," she said.

"Yes," said Mrs. Barron. She reached into her own purse and brought out the hairbrush. It was plastic, red with silver flecks like frozen snow. She handed it to the applicant. Mrs. Barron could not identify the expression on her face—then she could. Mrs. Gold was, she thought, grateful for the hairbrush.

"Now what?" asked Ms. Gold.

Mrs. Barron did not know what was next. She waited; she could barely breathe.

"Well. Thank you," said Ms. Gold, hesitantly.

Mrs. Barron closed her eyes for a moment. When she opened them, she saw Ms. Gold brushing her hair with the hairbrush. She brushed one side, and then another, carefully moving from front to back. Mrs. Barron thought that Ms. Gold was watching her for direction, it seemed, to do this task the correct way. She thought it was important not to tell the applicant anything. Then Ms. Gold handed the hairbrush back.

Mrs. Barron took it. "Thank you," she said. She was grateful to Ms. Gold for brushing her hair. This frightened her, a gratitude for this action, toward this stranger who resembled her daughter. Mrs. Barron even thought she loved the applicant, which was embarrassing. She was afraid she would step out from behind her desk and embrace her. The impulse was so strong to release this love, thwarted in her, that she felt a little faint. But she could not bend this woman into being her daughter; this fact made her understand that she could not possibly hire Ms. Gold. The applicant had done just what she requested, but in doing this had revealed the broad, vast expanse of Mrs. Barron's own sorrow.

"Your clips are excellent and you would be a great fit for our publication," said Mrs. Barron. "We have your information and we'll be in touch."

She stood up and they shook hands.

"Thank you," said the applicant, and paused. The applicant picked up her purse and turned toward the door. She touched her hair, gently, so Mrs. Barron had to look away.

Ms. Gold walked onto the bright street. The last thing the interviewer said made her understand. *We'll be in touch.* That was a no. She knew it, somehow, knew it with the firm grasp of her handshake, a kind of regret in its exaggerated firmness. Overcompensating for doubt. Had she not brushed her hair the correct way? If a man had asked her to do this, she would have walked out, she realized—why would a man hand her a brush? What condescension would that action reveal? But the way the woman asked her, and the way Mrs. Barron handed the brush to her, made Ms. Gold feel, oddly, taken care of for a moment.

She didn't know why that was important to her.

She realized how no one, not her friends, not her sister in Florida nor her cousins in Vermont, knew how she felt, sitting in front of the interviewer's desk. All of the interviewers behaved as though she were a person; they glanced at her résumé and asked her questions and decided whether she was the correct one or not, if she fit their needs, and she stood up and smiled and shook hands and left and never saw them again. She was a person, she knew that, a capable one, but she felt more and more like a shell, her skin cracking thin over nothing but air.

There was the sight of the hand holding out this ridiculous item, the hairbrush.

It was not an insult; it had not felt like one. When Mrs. Barron handed her the hairbrush, it seemed that the interviewer thought she was important somehow—real.

Ms. Gold paused. After interviews, she sometimes glanced at her résumé to check the precise diagram of her life; though the list of her experience never revealed anything new, the fact of the structure itself comforted her.

The sidewalks blazed pale before her, under an empty blue sky. She was walking to her final interview.

Mr. Holland thought he should cancel the interview. He stood up and closed the blinds. He needed to sit, for a moment, in the bluish shadows of his office.

He thought the doctor was, at first, telling him a joke. He would say what he said and then, with a pause, add, *Kidding!* But there had been no laughter, and there was the mention of prognosis and time. His body told him nothing. There was nothing but a constant sour throb in his stomach, not even that bad.

He could not believe he was sitting in this chair, sitting still. He thought he should get up, walk out of the office, take the elevator and run out of the building, into the cool air out side, hail a cab to the airport. He imagined looking at the list of cities: Paris, Taipei, New Delhi, Moscow. His palms were damp and he wiped them on his jacket. But assertion would do nothing. He was sitting here, at his desk, ridiculously wait- ing for this interview. And if he hired this person, six months later he would, probably, be dead.

Mr. Holland's office chair was a gray swivel chair with coffee stains. It would belong to someone else.

He pressed the buzzer for his secretary, about to tell her to cancel, but she said, "Oh, Mr. Holland, she's here! I'm sending her in."

And here was the applicant, rushing into the bizarre, hopeful country of employment, holding out her hand.

"I'm thrilled to be here," she said.

He felt his hand lift to reach hers. She grasped it and he registered her surprise at his nervousness, but he was glad in a way, she could detect his heart in his hand, the warm damp- ness of his palm.

"I've read *Metro Daily* for years," she said.

She had the peculiar honor of being the first person to see him since he received the news. But she would never know this. Her résumé was, somehow, on his desk, as he had been reading it before the doctor called.

He thought he had the right to tell her to get out. She was here under the illusion that she had a future. Who were they, the idiots that believed this? Who needed anyone's enthusiasm? He could barely look at her, sitting there. He did not want to be asking her questions.

In fact, he thought, *she* should be asking him.

"Ms. Gold," he said, and he felt he was hearing his voice for the first time. Was this how he sounded his whole life? A faint Brooklyn accent. He hated the way he pronounced a *G*.

He had a thought.

"We have our applicants ask the questions," he said. He leaned back in his chair, trying to appear relaxed.

"What kind of questions?"

"Ask them about me."

"About you?"

"Yes."

It didn't matter if she thought he was crazy. It didn't matter at all, he thought. He wanted to hear his own answers, not hers.

She stared at the floor for a moment, as though her question were located in the linoleum. Then she looked at him.

"What is most rewarding about this position?" she asked.

"Very little," he said. "Most of the copy is shitty. The people are crap. I've been here thirty years and I still watch my back. I have years of overtime, and you know what? I've never seen a dime."

Did he just say that? A sort of joy, like gray sunlight, flashed through him. He could say whatever he wanted. She

glanced at the door as though she believed there was somewhere else to go. But there was nowhere to go, he wanted to
tell her, not the waiting room, not the elevator, not the lobby,
not the other office buildings. Where did she think she could
walk to, in this world? Nowhere. Each moment was a room,
protecting him.

"What is the most important thing for a new employee to
know?"

"Watch out for Mr. Johnson. He'll flatter you and then try
to grab you by the coffee machine. And the junior reporters,
give them some of your takeout when you're here late or they'll
get surly. Starving, all of them. They're paid crap."

She sighed, sharply. "Is this really—"

"Ask me more," he said.

"Mr. Holland," she said, "I'm sorry, but I don't understand
the—"

"Please continue, Ms. Gold."

She regarded him with a fierce, probing expression, one
that would have made him uncomfortable other times, but he
found himself now welcoming it; her gaze seemed oddly kind.
He was a large man, late sixties, a stiff swath of gray hair. He
wanted her to see everything, to perceive every cell in his body,
his elbows, his fingernails, his eyelashes. He wished she, or
anyone, would memorize him.

"How long is your commute?" she asked.

"Fifty-five minutes. If the trains come on time. I'm coming in from Queens. Before, it was shorter, twenty minutes."

"Why was it shorter?"

"I was in Murray Hill. Rent-controlled apartment. My ex grabbed it. That place was nine hundred square feet, one thousand a month. A view of the East River. Now you don't want to know what I look out at."

"What?" she asked.

Some days, he didn't mind the view from his studio, the narrow brick alley between his building and the next. He heard the yelling of the family across the alley, and he valued the silence in his room. Other days, he felt the quiet of the room as a weight crushing him.

"Nothing," he said. His heart thrummed in his chest.

"Why didn't Elaine love me enough?" he said. "Ask me."

"Is that really—"

"Go ahead."

"Why did . . ." She paused. "Why didn't Elaine love you enough?"

"Excellent question," he said. "I thought I was a good enough guy."

"What do you mean?" she asked, her voice annoyed.

What was good enough? Now he thought of anyone who paid him any attention at all. The girl who smiled at him at the subway booth, that was something, wasn't it? His cousin who sometimes dropped by to make martinis for him. But before this, before the hoarding of any interaction, he had wanted more—he wanted to touch his wife more than she wanted to touch him, he wanted her asleep beside him every night, her hair, the sweet, dour coffee smell of her breath.

"How did you know you were good enough?"

He was not expecting her question. She was observant now, in an annoying and thorough way, sitting up, ready to take notes. He felt sorry for her.

"Who was it that left you? Girlfriend, wife, partner, what?"

"Wife," he said; he had not said the word in some time.

She clapped her palms together and regarded him.

"What did she want from you?" she asked.

"How should I know? I was better-looking when she married me. My apartment? Not kids, she didn't want them. Not money, I never had any." He looked around the office, taking in its feeling of crowded scarcity—there were piles of papers and books on chairs around the desk, but no photos, nothing on the walls. Panic was a silver line through his chest; he thought it might unzip him.

"Are you all right?" she asked.

"Yes," he said. He touched his forehead. "Just go on."

"I'm not sure what to ask now," she said.

"Ask me about my past," he said.

"What do you consider your greatest accomplishment?" she asked.

He could tell that she still, foolishly, thought this was an interview; she was trying to flatter him.

"Maybe I should have been a lawyer. Or a poet. Or a botanist. Maybe I lived the wrong damn life—"

They looked at each other and their gaze held the same fear. Ms. Gold firmly put her hand on his desk.

"Stop," she said. "You have answered enough. Let me answer some questions," she said.

He stared at her.

"All right," he said.

He looked out the window of his office; the mirrored buildings being constructed across the street, the crappy gray blinds in his office, the blue sky, everything was receding from him. Soon it would all vanish. But when he was gone, what would the world be?

Suddenly, he made a decision.

"You have the job," he said.

This was not true—he did not know why he said it. He didn't even have the power to decide this, but he said it anyway. She blinked hard, as though he had thrown water into her eyes.

"I don't believe you," she said.

"Why not?"

"You can't decide just like that. You have procedures, Human Resources—"

"I'll hire you," he said. "I'll hire you and your sister and your mother and your father and your lover and your children, I'll just hire them all—"

He wanted to, sincerely, then. Maybe he was this— generous! This new feeling, this abundance made him feel lighter. He wanted to bring her on board.

"I don't believe you," she said. "This is too quick."

"You're hired!" he said, realizing the more he repeated it, the less convincing it sounded. "Did you hear that? You're a reporter at *Metro Daily*. You're hired."

She looked so tall, now, standing up, though she was not

even that tall a person, but appeared now completely different—like a tree.

"Really?" she asked, briskly. "Hand me the paperwork. I'll
do it now."

He didn't have any paperwork. She waited for a long moment, and then, obviously, she knew. "Come on," she said. "I
don't need any more bullshit. What the hell is wrong with all
of you? I need something real." She picked up her purse.

"Wait," he said.

He stood up and walked around his desk, so he was facing her.

"I just want to ask you—" he said.

She set her purse on her shoulder and stepped back from
him. He was standing in front of her; he could smell his own
odor, which was rotting and bitter.

"I have to go—" she said.

"Wait," he said. "Wait."

He could hear his own heart in his chest, its ridiculous
song.

"Are you okay?" she asked him.

She was about to leave, watching him.

He knew that, in a minute or so, she would leave for her
next appointment. She would take the elevator to the lobby,
walk through the revolving doors to the street, fade into the
crowd. He would never see her again. He had already forgotten her name.

"A pleasure to meet you," she said, which was clearly a lie,
and she held out her hand, as though this was actually a job

interview. The gesture moved him in a way that surprised him. He shook her hand, but there was no energy in his handshake, and he knew she could feel that; he wondered what else she could tell.

She turned to leave. "Wait," he said, softly, so she would not hear. He stood, uncertain, in front of her, and tried to figure out what he wanted to say.

Ms. Gold walked out onto the bright street. The late afternoon glare reflected off the glass of the skyscrapers so they looked as if they were made of sun. People rushed around her, each one with a place to belong. She felt a flash of love for all of them— the businessman, the nurse in scrubs, the cabdriver, the hot dog vendor; she wanted to grab any one and become them. She was so tired; she did not want to be herself. There were so many disappointments. She had done three interviews today, more than she had done in weeks; she doubted any would lead to a job.

She was impatient, wanting answers. What was the key? What could she have done differently? Perhaps she should have bought the jacket. Perhaps she should have used the Cambria font on her résumé instead of Helvetica. Perhaps she should have walked down another street when she met the last man she loved. Perhaps she should have listened to her parents. Perhaps she should not have moved away from her place of birth, or perhaps she should have. She wanted to know the mistake, the moment that would explain everything to her. She stopped on the sidewalk, people flowing around her. A man bumped against her and he muttered something. She did not care. She did not move because she was thinking. She was thinking. The buildings loomed, large boxes of light. She wanted, for a moment, to run back and ask Mr. Holland one more question; then she kept walking.

The New Order

We were friends, or we knew each other, and both of us had been in the other room when the attack occurred. This was in the 1970s, when these events didn't happen at schools. A teacher and a ninth grader were shot in the cafeteria and another teacher was injured so that, from then on, her arm hung down like a broken wing. The girl who was killed was a member of the cello section, and she was named Sandra. We were all part of the Intermediate Orchestra of our junior high school, and she had been in the cafeteria, where we were also supposed to be ten minutes after she had left the multipurpose room. The cafeteria was serving fish and chips and Sandra left early because she wanted to be first in line. The man went to the table and shot two teachers and also her, one, two, three, everyone looking on, in disbelief; the man had been one of the fathers at the school.

As part of the process to get us past the incident, which was what they called the attack, after the assemblies, and the short and not fruitful discussions in homeroom telling us to report any suspicious behavior to the vice principal, our orchestra teacher, Mr. Handelman, decided to proceed as usual. In two weeks we were supposed to audition for our chairs in the orchestra. We would each play for one minute and the teacher would rank us on tone, musicality, and pitch, and arrange us in a new order.

Lori and I had become, strangely, better friends after the incident. We didn't know Sandra very well—mostly we knew her as a good cellist. She had a deep tone that you could hear in your stomach, when she played, that made the air feel like velvet. She usually occupied Seat Three. Lori was Seat Two. She had always been Seat Two. Seat One went to John Schubert, who was adept at pieces that required rapid finger work, whose thumb slid buttery up the strings and who was always, in a way that seemed almost supernatural, on key, but whose tone was sometimes thin, as though revealing some deep unsolved craving within him. We all regarded each other with sharp, interested eyes.

The new order was especially important because the first cello would perform a short, one-minute solo as part of a fall festival performance for the school. In the center of my heart, I wanted to be Seat One someday. I practiced a lot. I was going to audition with my favorite piece, "The Dying Swan," which felt perhaps problematic, but it was what I was best at playing, and I loved how I felt when I played it—my chest pressing against the wood of the cello, the sense that I was inside the music, which felt like the heart of everything, and, at that age, I wanted to crouch inside the heart of the world.

I tried not to think about Sandra or the teachers when we sat in the cafeteria. We had not been allowed in it for a week as the school administration scrubbed any evidence of the incident from the room, but, unfortunately, there was nowhere else to feed us, so they let us back in. The room was now clean in a stringent, terrifying way, as though it represented all the thoughts we were not supposed to have about our futures. There were rumors about the incident. Everyone wanted to have a theory. Sandra had been wearing a tube top, and the murderous father instructed his daughter, a ninth grader named Jen, not to wear tube tops; he was rumored to find them immodest and harmful in some way no one could explain. Or he shot at Mrs. Simon, an algebra teacher, who had recently turned him down for a date, and Sandra, unfortunately, just got in the way. There was no clarity on anything (as though there could be), but the cloudiness of the incident made everyone eager to contribute to the memorial the school now set up in a corner, a peculiar display with a few bouquets of flowers, some posters with large hearts drawn on them. Everyone was eager to show a capacity for love.

We talked about the other members of the orchestra with an intense desire to categorize them, sort them in ways that were flattering and not. Lori assumed a new mantle of authority following the attack, a new hardness that made it seem she wanted to press herself like a bug into amber, into the air. I looked at Lori and I wanted to fold myself into her, which was an impulse that alarmed me; I didn't know why I thought I would be safe in her; I wanted her, or someone in the world, to locate me. I wanted this so much I was dizzy. We glanced at the teachers, the other students, wondering who might kill us. It could be anyone, apparently, and it was unclear what could be the armor to stop it.

In this realm of anxiety, we briskly, authoritatively, ranked the others. We agreed that John was overrated in his playing but had a beautiful way of spinning the cello when he was bored, his long legs stretched out, and that Tracy L. in the flute section was a bad player because her high notes never quite hit the right way.

Lori called her mother a loser; her parents divorced, mother always out, or her mother's girlfriends coming over and all of them drinking vodka shots in the car. My parents were always home, but moved as if the air were made of Jell-O, and they believed the world was always about to break. We sat in that gleaming, scrubbed cafeteria and ate our sugary hamburgers. The world was trembling around us, and it seemed it was going to eat us. We did not talk about the incident. We did not talk about everything we did each day to our classmates in our minds, for the boundary between the violence outside and inside our minds seemed thin and permeable; routinely I would be murdering an unbearable violinist who gave me cold, diminishing looks, or pressing myself naked against the first clarinetist who had delicate, beautiful arms I wanted to wrap around me; I wanted so much, always; the world was spangled and nothing felt quite real.

Lori talked on and on about the mundane, about the Corkys shoes she desired and the way she glared at the boy who once spit at her when she didn't say hi back and the way the square of chocolate cake the cafeteria served today tasted like metal, which seemed unfortunate and wrong. I wanted her to help me so fiercely my skin burned. I wanted someone to help me.

Now we sat in that cafeteria, our lunches set out on the table, the hamburger and frozen fries and pudding separated into their little compartments, and we pretended we were merely eating, that we were safe. The theater of the two of us continuing convinced me, a little. I believe Lori felt this, too.

We both wanted to be first cello, to perform that solo, to play for a moment in a circle of brightness. We discussed the upcoming auditions for our new chairs carefully, not sharing what music we would audition with. Lori seemed particularly nervous, which was curious to me, for she was a good player, her tone better than anyone's. She stretched and said, "I'm so bad. I'm going to fuck up," a groan that was a lie, because she was better than I was, talented in an ineffable, natural way, and I understood that my role was to say to her, "No, you're not going to," which felt like opening my mouth too wide. And I was filled with a chilly, unruly fear. For this was the true thing: we both wanted to be first chair and perform that solo. We were both shouldering darkness, in that hot, dirty cafeteria, but what we wanted was a moment in the light, the auditorium filled with people listening to us play the music of composers who created these sounds two hundred years ago. We sat in the cafeteria, the other kids shouting to each other across the room, screaming. We wanted to taste those hamburgers forever; we wanted to live.

We had two weeks to practice. The entire orchestra was practicing. I walked by little practice rooms and heard the muffled sounds of violins, cellos, oboes, flutes, the intent sounds of students. Inside these rooms, everyone sounded angelic and furious. I imagined the students had lost their voices and could now only speak through their instruments, like this. I walked by a room and heard Lori practicing and stood, my heart lacy with panic, by her door.

In those days after the incident, we were different. We were all afraid. There was the way we all jolted up when the alarm system in the school went off, the false alarms that were a guttural, metronome sound. The way we all held our breath. The way the teachers walked down the corridors and could break into a run at any moment. The way it seemed the steel tables could lift off the linoleum floor.

Eating our lunch, we eyed each other like vultures. We were flying over the world, hovering, ready to dive in and grab what we needed. We were talking about our pieces and what we would play and Lori's arm stretched out on the chair beside her and she was describing I don't know what, the fact that her bow didn't take resin well, or that again she thought she would fail during her solo, saying this again, when we both knew it wasn't true. It felt false in an elaborate, manufactured way, made in a factory of lies, and this made me furious. I was furious at the way the school had not told us exactly why the father had gone on his rampage, or I was furious at the lame directions they gave us, to hit the ground if someone else did this, which I knew wouldn't help a thing. I was furious at the way my parents or the school told us not to worry. I was furious when Lori claimed she would perform badly when she knew music so naturally and fully she would not. There was a flash of violence outside of me and within me, a massive truck driving over and through my skin.

"You won't win," I said. It just came out. There was no reason to say it. I just did.

I paused. Then I continued—"No one thinks you'll win."

She stared at me. She lifted a trembling hand to brush hair off her face.

"Why not?" she asked, softly.

"People just say. Lots of people. No way."

This was getting worse by the moment. I looked away. I felt a pressure in my throat, the capacity to say more and more.

"What people?"

"Many. I can't say."

This seemed the worst thing, the manufacture of others demeaning her. But I stood by this. I didn't know how to stop.

"Well," she said. She was unable to look at me. I felt powerful for the first time since the incident, as though I had become a steel spike, completely hard and sharp; but I also trembled, for I simultaneously felt a plunging sense of loss. It was confusing to experience both of these at once. I realized then how much I admired my friend, even loved her, and that I had damaged something I could not see. Lori didn't stand up and walk away; she changed the subject to the staleness of the carrot cake on our plates, but it felt as though something finished between us, and that we were now unknowable to one another, separate, an ostrich and a bear.

We auditioned for our seats, all of us, in the room where the orchestra met, and we perched on metal chairs and listened to each other play. It took two hours to go through all of us, our teacher listening with a blank face, his eyelids quivering when he heard music that was startling or good. The violinists went, the flautists, the French horn section, the cellos. We were middle school students, the harshest audience in the world. My playing flew by; I imagined I was housed within the music, and, perhaps, briefly I was. But when I finished, my hand was trembling. I barely heard the music I played.

I sat in the back and listened as the other cellists performed; one by one, each carved their particular song into the air. Lori's tone swelled dark and lovely into the room, and I was listening, knowing that she had beaten me with that tone, revealing some deep honeyed quality in herself—for the music, when played the right way, seemed to reveal a hidden internal beauty that, previously, no one could see. That was the most glorious feature of the orchestra, the surprising revelations of beauty from people who might be shallow or petty in everyday life. We were just sitting there in that grubby room and it would happen, a floating ribbon of sound. It was better than all of us. Some of the best players knew this and were coy about it. They rushed some golden thing off their violin or flute or trumpet and then gazed into the distance as though they had announced: *See. Here.*

I clutched my cello, feeling more sick by the moment due to a variety of things: the peculiar fact that, two weeks after the attack, we were continuing this process at all, which felt both cruel and a relief, the fact that I wanted to be first chair so much I could barely breathe, the fact that I wished, beyond anything, that I could play like Lori, and that I had ruined something between us by my spite.

And then there was a squawk of her bow. A bleat.

We all heard it—the inside of her skin had been turned out, and for a moment all of ours had as well. Her face twitched. She continued. It was shocking. Lori never made mistakes.

She did not look at anyone when she had finished, though I watched her, wanting to catch her eye, to be absolved of the awful fact: I made her mess up. It was a fact that was as clear to me as the sky. I had helped her doubt herself so she made this mistake, and suddenly I wanted to comfort her, in some sorry soft part of myself, but she put away her cello, picked up her backpack, and walked out.

• • •

They announced the new order the next day. Mr. Handelman tallied everyone's score and read out where we were. The class was quiet for once. He announced violins, violas.

The order of these sections resembled what it had been before.

Then he announced the order of the cello section. We sat and waited to be called.

He said my name. First.

I looked up. How could this be? He glanced at me, nodded. "You played well," he said, acknowledging all of our surprise. I could feel shock flicker across the faces of other cellists. I was now Seat One. It felt at the same time wrong and also completely predictable, clicking into a buried hope I held about myself. I felt like I contained a thousand golden coins. After he read the names, we shifted into our new seats. I carried my cello to the first seat and sat down. I looked at the others and they seemed very far away, even though they were all just a few feet beside me, and John Schubert right beside me. The sun had come up in the wrong part of the sky.

After her disastrous audition, Lori now occupied the seventh chair out of eight. We did not know how to look at each other. I had won but I hadn't. There was now a piece of rotten fruit in the room. I wondered if there was any way to actually win, to ascend to some place of calm and triumph, but perhaps there was not. There was no way to win. This thought scared me so much I tried to think of one word, like "red" or "sneaker," over and over, because I did not want to be thinking about this at all.

Sometimes Lori's particular, deep tone rose through the others. I loved her tone. I wanted to inhabit it. I tried to send this message to her in my mind, my admiration of it. Our conversations were different now, and we mostly used the word "fine." We were speaking another language entirely. Then she dropped out of orchestra and I didn't see her at all.

I prepared for my solo. I practiced a lot, and our teacher nodded at me in a way that said he thought I could do it. But right before the concert, there was a slight earthquake and the auditorium where we were supposed to perform was damaged. The concert was canceled, forever.

A week later, we auditioned again for a holiday concert. This time, when I auditioned, I slipped down to seventh chair. I sat in the same chair Lori held before she left.

We threw our caps into the sky. We ran into each other on the wide, grassy field where we graduated junior high, filled with hundreds of ninth graders and their parents, the grass trampled by a thousand shoes. Lori's parents were walking carefully, distant from each other, her mother shouting something to her father. Lori walked in front of them, clutching a bouquet of balloons, her face squinting as though the afternoon light had suddenly become too much. I raised my hand to wave at her, low enough so that if she wanted to ignore me, I could pretend I was scratching my face. She saw me and raised her hand the same way, and for one moment we were looking at each other, with no expression I could categorize—then we kept walking, past each other, and on.

We went to high school. Lori was districted for another school, so she vanished. Whenever I met someone from her school I asked if they knew her and found out various facts— that she was dating a football player, that she crashed her mother's car, that she was working at Hardee's. Then I heard nothing. Sometimes I passed Sandra's older brother in our high school. He was on the basketball team, and walked with a loose, loping pace. Once I saw him pack up his belongings as he left his trigonometry class, and I was impressed by the way he organized his backpack, the tenderness with which he slid each notebook inside.

The teacher whose arm had been injured in the incident was transferred to the high school I attended. She taught and sometimes told stories about the moment she saw the father run into the cafeteria. She kept thinking he wanted to eat the food being served that day. Why else would someone come to the cafeteria? What other reason could there be? She often said that and sighed, and gently touched her wounded arm.

• • •

My life unfolded in ways that surprised me and did not. I stopped playing cello in high school, but that time in the orchestra left an echo—this fierce gleam of desire. The desire took various forms. It fell like a pale net over anything I could capture. It fell over people. It fell over a man who loved me for the way I kissed him and then thought I had the wrong taste; the man who admired me as long as I didn't contribute more sentences to a conversation than he did; the man who loved the least pretty parts of me, loved my feet and legs, who I wanted to crawl inside because he seemed like a shelter, until he was not. We moved with the family to many cities over the years, and the net fell over each city as I tried to find a way to make it a home. It fell over my children, who appeared one way when I dreamed of them and another way when they arrived, who accepted my love but then were affronted by it, who believed I could offer nothing to them and rushed away. It fell over goals for work. I studied in my desired field, I took tests and failed them and took them again; but when I went from interview to interview there was something in my face, something lurking in the way I sat, that made them turn away. It fell over me as I walked down the street, as I walked by men I hoped would look at me and ones I hoped would not, it fell over my body, various days, as I tried to protect it—when that guy who came to fix the washer kept calling and telling me he would show up at any moment, when that boss somehow figured out where I lived and kept following me home, leaving oddly chosen gifts in my mailbox, the pink plush bunny, the Toblerone bar, until the day he whispered to me by the Xerox machine, *bitch you didn't thank me*, and I quit the job and moved away.

There were many types of violence in the world, some quieter. I walked down the street and I imagined if the pounding I felt, in different forms each day, existed within me or outside of me. Had I done something? Or was this the way everything was supposed to be? How did you make your way through the world dodging the violence both outside and within? There was, in me, a continual restlessness, a move-ment, a wondering.

I was forty, then fifty. I never sold my cello, but I never played it either; it was in a closet, packed away. One day, I picked up the cello and played a few notes. It sounded terrible. I could hold my bow, but to pull the bow across the strings felt awkward. I could not move it with the right pressure. I could not believe that I was ever capable of making a sound that was like velvet or honey.

I sometimes thought about Lori, and the way we talked about that audition, the way we had all waited, frozen, for our chance to play, and how we fell, so quickly, into that new order. How the process of making that order once seemed the most significant event in the world, and how I now understood its brevity. How I wanted to be important, and how I wanted to be alive. I thought of the feeling that rose up, sharply, when I told her she wouldn't win. How I felt like a spike. I was both appalled by and enjoyed that feeling.

During my life, I said things I wished I hadn't. I stormed out of rooms, I ruined things with others, I acted foolishly and without thinking, I did things I don't want to admit, actions that filled me with shame, but that moment was somehow the one I remembered.

Then, one day, she called me.

I was in the neighborhood, she said. I looked you up.

It was her voice. It sounded like her regular voice, from forty years ago, but also like it had been put through a strange, bleary horn.

"You may not remember me. I'm Lori Longstreet. From Garfield Junior High?"

Her voice trembled, but I knew it.

"From Advanced Orchestra?"

It still was somehow important, to me, that it was Advanced.

"It's me!"

She sounded delighted to be found. She was passing through the city where I lived, and she wanted to stop by. She was trying to see some old friends.

Old friends—she said it as if we had rollicked through school together. I thought of our sitting in the cafeteria, and wondered if she remembered exactly who I was.

I said I would be delighted to see her. I was. I wondered if she needed a place to stay.

She hesitated. That would be helpful, she said.

I lived alone in a rental then, a small house with blue vinyl siding that somewhat resembled wood. In the back, a deck overlooked a small yard, and during the spring, the azaleas rose, a pink and foamy tide. There was a spare room; my children didn't visit often. So just like that, Lori was going to come by.

I needed to get the place ready. I wasn't someone who loved cleaning, but it seemed important to clean the house. I vacuumed, I scrubbed the counters, I wiped smudges off walls. I noticed the crack in the window I never seemed to get fixed, and the peeling paint where the kitchen ceiling leaked. I noticed everything that was wrong. I rarely looked that closely at this place where I slept and ate, but when I did, I found extensive stains, odd smears. I understood that I mostly moved through my life trying not to look at them.

In the bathroom, I peered at myself in the mirror and haplessly rubbed moisturizer into my face. What would she see when she saw me? Would she remember what I had said? I remembered my words, how powerful I felt after they left my mouth, and how sour it became after I said them. The way we sat at the steel tables in the cafeteria, the way we negotiated our confusion and shame at being alive, the way we tried to believe in our claim to this air, these tables, these hamburgers before us, sitting on those hard steel benches, so cold they seemed to be balanced on ice.

She arrived in the afternoon. I saw her get out of a cab slowly. At first, I didn't think I was looking at Lori at all, but at her mother. Her hair was now cut short and silver, in a bob. She had slipped into the body of her mother like it was a coat. It was always a surprise to experience this in people you hadn't seen in a long time. But I pretended not to see any shift in her, as I knew she would pretend not to see any in me. I stepped out into the sunlight and waved.

"Hello!" she called. I hurried to the sidewalk to meet her. She hugged me, a firm hug, which was a change—she was not the type who hugged before. Her hair held the smell of a meadow, and I remembered how wildflower shampoo was her favorite many years ago. I felt the solidity of her arms.

We walked up to the house; she dragged a small suitcase behind her. She walked with care. I could see her fourteen-year-old face housed in her middle-aged face, which was the gift that friends from your youth gave you—they could locate the particular beauty in you from decades before, and you could locate it in them.

I wanted her approval. This nervousness surprised me, and I tried not to show it to her.

I opened the door and she stepped inside. I eyed my possessions critically, apprising what was there. A bamboo lamp stand, a porcelain lamp from my grandmother, a turquoise pillow with drawings my children had silk-screened on them, for an elementary school fund-raiser. Lori walked in, placing her feet guardedly on the floor, and her expression held the same authority as her younger self, but was now overlaid with something else, a gauze-like film of calm.

"I like your house," she said. "Look at this."

She walked around, brushing her fingers against items in the living room—the lamp, the coffee table, a blue glass vase.

She talked. She talked a lot about nothing. It seemed to

me that she was nervous, but the quality of her talking was not anxious, but simply had the purpose of filling the air. She liked admiring things, in that nervous way people have when they want to establish intimacy quickly. She sat on the couch and stretched out her legs. She admired the potted geraniums, the strawberries I put in a dish as a snack. There was a self-absorbed quality to the admiration, as if she wanted me to approve of her. She had been in contact with many people from our junior high school: a month ago, she ran into John Schubert, the best cellist, by the avocados at Ralph's supermarket. John told her about his experience as a music major at UCLA, which ended abruptly when he broke his wrist during a softball game; he now managed an instrument store in West Covina.

I remembered the low roar of that multipurpose room, all of us talking as we perched on our fold-out chairs. Mr. Handelman clapped and we picked up our instruments, and looked to him, waiting for him to begin conducting. That building no longer existed; it had been knocked down years ago to make room for a new basketball court.

"What do you think Mr. Handelman is doing now?" I asked. "Is he still teaching?"

Her face stilled.

"Oh," she said, looking at me. "Don't you know? Mr. Handelman had a heart attack last year. He was teaching until the last minute, and then, boom, he died."

My heart jumped in the way it did when I heard bad news. "Oh," I said.

She wore the same expression she had when she was fourteen and knew information that I didn't, as though her knowledge put her on a shelf above me. She had not lost this capacity.

"I thought you knew," she said.

"I didn't," I said.

"Well," she said. "I'm sorry. Let me tell you some good news, then—remember the trumpet section? Gail and Harold? They got married. And they play for a band in a circus. In Austria! They have an exciting life—"

I wished there was something I could tell her that she didn't know. But she sat in my living room, glowing almost, with her expansive knowledge of what everyone else was doing.

She kept talking. She was celebrating her twenty-sixth year of marriage with her husband, Fred, who was her best friend, and she was now an aficionado of French cooking and made excellent soufflés, and on her fiftieth birthday, her children threw a party for her at a restaurant on the Marina, just on their own, without her asking, and on and on. She did not sound like she was bragging, though of course she was, but I heard something else in her tone, what I knew of her from junior high school—the sense that she was asking permission, from me.

I listened. I could see that she was glad I was listening. We had tea, and then I made pasta with broccoli and garlic and Parmesan for dinner. We sat, facing each other at the table, the way we used to in the cafeteria. I wondered if she thought I looked old, my hand placed carefully on my cheek to conceal any weary parts of my face. She thought that everything I prepared was delicious.

"I could eat this forever," she said. "I want the recipe."

She even got a little card out of her purse and wrote it down, right then. When she brushed her hair from her face, it was an adult gesture echoing the way she did this as a child.

Her appreciation was nice, but I felt a kind of force behind her comments, a radiation, lifting off an explosion within. It made me want to duck under something. I kept peering at her, waiting for her to do something that would instantly reveal her adolescent self; I longed to see the authority she once had.

My response was to keep feeding her. After the pasta, more strawberries. Then some mint chip ice cream, which had been sitting in the freezer for so long there was a sheen of ice on the top.

Our conversation circled, floated around the room. But the discussion wasn't answering some important questions. Did she ever play cello anymore? Did she remember playing in the orchestra? What else did she remember?

I wasn't sure what I wanted her to say, but I wanted the past to be simpler than I remembered.

Her face flickered. "Oh, orchestra," she said. "I stopped playing right after I dropped out. I just didn't want to. I didn't want to touch a cello after, everything."

She clasped her hands in front of her, firmly, as though she were being interviewed in some legal way.

I felt a sadness settle in me, entwined with guilt.

"But you were so good," I said, wanting her to know this, "I remember your tone. It was better than anyone's—"

"I was okay," she said, noticing my expression. "I didn't want to play anymore. Maybe I should have. But I just didn't.

Something was there in me, I wanted to do something else. I had so much energy. You know? I tried running. I joined the track team. I ran with other girls for six miles until I couldn't breathe. I wanted to run farther, until I hurt my knee. Then I went through a time when I was sleeping with a lot of different guys. Some I liked, some I didn't, but I just wanted to feel how they made me feel, in every way possible. I learned a lot during that time. I still wanted things. After that, I started baking cakes. I wanted to make the best cakes, the sweetest. Then I gained forty pounds because I kept eating them. Each cake was more delicious than the other, and I had to finish them all. Then I started going to spin classes, and I dropped twenty pounds."

She sat back, exhausted.

"In the last year or so," she said, "I haven't been well. I won't go into the boring details, because I'm sick of talking about them, but, well. This stupid body. Now while I can still get around, I wanted to see everyone I knew."

I looked at Lori, a slight chill inside me. There was nothing that appeared different about her, except for the careful way she walked. I peered at her, trying to figure it out.

"Oh," I said, saying the things one said when confronted with vague medical information, "I didn't know. I'm sorry—"

She waved these words away. She closed her eyes.

"Whatever."

"What—" I said. "Do you need anything? Are you—"

"Let me show you pictures of the cakes," she said.

She held out her phone, showing me photos of cakes she had made when she inhabited that particular expression of longing. The cakes were round, decorated with various types of perfectly formed, bright flowers, and, even if the cakes were iced in yellows and pinks, had the odd feeling of fortresses.

Finally, after talking for several hours, I told her I had to go to sleep; I showed her the room with her bed and her towels. Then I shut the door to my room and thought of her in the other room, and I had a sudden thought that she would open my door, march into the room, and stab me. I imagined the compliments about my pasta were all a front, that she had been waiting all these years, secretly, to do this. I could picture her standing over me, taking clear aim for my heart. I didn't know why this idea came to me, but the more I thought it the more possible it seemed. I lay in the darkness for some time, listening for movement, but there was none. I locked the door.

In the morning, I woke up and, for a moment, did not get out of bed. I listened to Lori, moving around the house. In the pale, morning light, I did not feel she would stab me, but was comforted by her presence. I wanted her to stay another night, and I also wondered why she was here at all.

When I came out of my room, she was sitting at the kitchen table drinking coffee.

"Hi!" she said. She had to leave at around two—and was heading home.

I brought out some rubbery croissants from Safeway and we sat together, the same way we sat at that cafeteria table forty years ago.

I thought of us then, the way we leaned toward each other needing the fact of our own presence, then the feeling that we were made of fog. I thought of the sound of my voice when I told her she wouldn't win, and the absolute steeliness of my whole self at that moment, the piercing of love between us, of our friendship. I took a bite of the horrible croissant.

"Lori," I said. "Have you heard anything about Sandra's family? What happened to them?"

It was not an honest question because I followed what had happened to them. The mother fell into depression, and they moved to Arizona. The older brother became a reporter on the local news in Phoenix. The father had a stroke a few years after the murder.

She put down her croissant. Her hand was a little shaky.

"I haven't," she said.

Then she told me this.

She had been annoyed at Sandra that morning. Sandra came into the orchestra room wearing a yellow tube top, and Lori felt a wilting inside because Sandra looked radiant in it, as though she had, through great will or knowledge, changed a deep force within herself. Sandra walked differently, more lightly when she wore it as well, as if she were balancing on a piece of sky. It was how some girls moved through the world now, with that precise assurance. But we were not those girls. Some were, but we were not. Lori told me that one reason she liked orchestra was not just because she enjoyed playing music but because she felt safe with that cello in front of her. It was like a large and kindly guard.

And here was Sandra in the tube top, her shoulders gleaming, Sandra walking and invisibly throwing glitter into the air. And then Lori felt certain that Sandra was going to crush her in some way she could not explain.

Lori wanted to get rid of her.

"Go," she told Sandra. "It's fish and chips day. Don't you want to be the first in line?"

Fish and chips were Sandra's favorite lunch. Everyone knew. Lori said that she remembered how Sandra looked at her, trying to figure out if leaving early was a good idea.

"Aren't you hungry?" Lori had said. "It'll be a long line."

She was doing her a favor, Lori told herself, telling her to go first in line. In fact, she was being generous to Sandra, helpful even, ignoring the fact that she was happy when Sandra ran off. Lori was glad, just then, that she didn't have to look at her. That clear feeling of relief. She didn't have to watch Sandra walk through the orchestra room and feel that she, herself, was somehow flawed. Lori thought she would follow her to the cafeteria, in ten minutes, but then Sandra would have disappeared into the crowd and Lori then believed that she would not feel diminished.

She remembered, later, how clear her mind was the ten minutes after Sandra left. The worry that had rushed through her was gone.

And then there was the slow unfurling of catastrophe, the shouting and the sound of alarms, and the fact that no one could go to lunch at all. Mr. Handelman shutting the doors and locking them, the news that something was happening in the cafeteria, not just lunch, and that some people had been injured. No, not just injured: killed.

We didn't hear that Sandra was dead until the next day, and this at first seemed a lie, a rumor, a joke, nothing that could be real.

Lori said that when she found out, she laughed—not because she thought it was funny, but because she had no idea what reaction to have. There was no sense to the statement that Sandra had been killed; nothing felt real at all. In fact, it seemed that her brain had shut down: she could not think. She could not believe this.

Lori spoke quickly and did not look at me as she told me all of this, the words surging with an intensity that made me wonder if this was the first time she was telling this story. And then she put her hand on mine and said,

"I want to thank you."

Her hand felt too cool, like a ghoul's.

"For what?"

"You understood," she said. "You said I wouldn't win."

She looked at me with an assumption of my innocence that was so utterly incorrect it felt as though the world was constructed of nothing. I had not understood anything; she was wrong. The absolute wrongness of this made me concerned and suddenly I wanted to eat everything in the world. I took a bite of croissant and chewed it, slowly. I wondered if I should just allow her this misunderstanding of me, for I came out in such a good light.

"I did say that," I said.

"I felt like my terrible nature was finally seen," she said. "And you were right. I shouldn't have been First Chair."

I picked up our plates and put them in the sink so I wouldn't have to look at her. Lori's face shone with certainty about the misguided fact of my goodness.

"*You* didn't shoot her," I said, carefully. "You just told her to get lunch. You didn't know—"

"So?" she said. Her eyes were bright and troubled. "I somehow helped. If she had not gone to the cafeteria, she would be here."

"Shut up," I said, trying to sound a little light, but she jumped. "What are you talking about?" I continued. "It was him. He did it. Not you."

"But I gave her the idea to go."

I stared at her. I had to tell her—that she was wrong about me, that the actual reason I told her she would not win was because I wanted to win, I wanted to play in the circle of light.

"But then I heard you play in the auditions," she said, "and I thought, she will be First Chair, I knew it before he said it, and then you were, and I felt somehow freed. I can't explain why. But I was glad that you had won, not me."

Just as I had felt forty years ago, sitting across from one another in that cafeteria, it seemed we were sitting on different continents. I waited for myself to correct her. I waited.

I did not.

On the continent across the table, she put her hands over her face and sighed. "So," she said. There was a silence between us that felt a thousand years old. She got up and stood, a little lost, in the kitchen. She went into the room where she had slept and wheeled out her suitcase. I followed her, and I felt needy; I wanted to talk to her more. I didn't want her to leave.

"Do you have a cello?" she asked.

I kept my old cello stored in the back of my closet with other items I didn't use. I brought it out and unzipped its vinyl bag. I had not played in many years; it made no sense to keep it, but I carried it everywhere I had lived. The strings were limp with disuse. They were soundless when you plucked them. She rubbed her palms on the curved top of the cello, the rounded edges of it.

"Do you ever play?" Lori asked.

"No," I said. "Never."

"But you still have it," she said.

I did. I refused to give it away.

"When was the last time you played?" I asked.

She thought. "I don't know. Thirty years ago?"

"I remember how you played," I said. I wanted to convince her of something, of the beauty of her sound. "I remember it."

She looked at the cello and rubbed her palm across the edges.

"May I try?" she asked.

"Yes," I said.

She tuned the old instrument so that it had some approximation of a cello, and then sat down in the living room and leaned its neck against her shoulder. She settled herself behind the instrument, turned the tuning pegs, plucked the strings and listened to them. I had forgotten what it was to play an instrument, to feel myself creating the clear notes, to feel the fluttering and hum of music against my chest, that gorgeousness rising from my arms, my breath.

I waited to tell her why I had said what I said to her. I waited.

She tightened the bow and drew it across the strings of the cello.

"How do I sound?" she asked.

I felt we had been talking since the beginning of the world. Outside, it was just after noon; soon the sun would start dying. A sparrow called. Somehow I knew that this was the last time I would see her. We sat across from each other, our chairs balanced on the flat, grubby carpet, sitting up, politely, our backs straight, trying to hold down this room with only our own weight. A million years ago, we sat in the cello section of Garfield Junior High's Advanced Orchestra; a million years ago, we sat on the cafeteria's cold steel benches, as, around us, our classmates roared. Lori's thin fingers touched the neck of the cello. She plucked the strings, A, D, G, C. They echoed in the small room. She set the bow on the strings and slowly drew it across them, and the two of us listened, waiting to hear the sound she made.

The Good Mothers
in the Parking Lot

They have not arrived. The parking lot is dark, and it is November and you are waiting for them and your arms feel hard as glass in the cold. You are at the elementary school and you are waiting for the other mothers; you are going to send your children off on a field trip. The bus is going to drive hours and hours through the night, bringing the children to a national park. Some of the parents are nervous; it is their first time sending their children away on a trip. The children are ten years old. It is three days after the election. The night is cold and the sky is black and starless and feels lower; the sky is weighted in a different way now, with grief. But this feels like a new, startling form of grief. The cars rumble into the dark parking lot one by one, making a crunching sound as they roll across the asphalt. The cars are big enough to kill a dozen people with one false turn. The clear pale brightness from the headlights swings across the dark emptiness of the parking lot, everyone standing here made brilliant for a moment, then their faces imperceptible, dim.

You have not seen these mothers since the election. You wait for the other mothers to get out of their cars, which roll in, one after another, no one unlocking their doors at first, peering out. Perhaps they are afraid too, or just cold, because it is November and now you can see your breath in the air. You wait. You wonder what each mother will look like now. You wonder if their faces will blind you, or if you will crumble when they step off the bus, or if they will even be able to look you in the eyes because they are suddenly surprised and ashamed. The asphalt in the parking lot may crumble into ash.

There is the sound of a crow, in the darkness, cawing.

None of these mothers talked about him before the election. No one put bumper stickers on their cars. Everyone here was very quiet about it. But you suspected. And you know who voted for whom from reports from the children, who listen to everything.

These are good mothers. You think of all of the ordinary activities you have done with these mothers over the years. All the playgrounds you have visited with them, all the hallways you sat in as you waited for dance classes to end, all the teachers you complained about, all the girls sleeping over at one house or another, the caramelness between mothers, the warmth connecting you and them as all of you tried to figure out how to be good mothers.

The car doors start to open.

Their children jump out first, just visible in the darkness, carrying their rolled-up sleeping bags to pack on the bus. Their children are eager for an adventure; their innocence makes them seem sugary, candied. They do not know how the world has changed. Then the mothers step out, slamming the car doors. First, the shadows of their bodies, opening the backs of the cars, lifting out duffel bags. You can't quite tell who is who in the darkness. The headlights beam bright swaths of light that make it hard, at first, to see their faces.

You are very still, watching. Other cars whisk by on the road, traveling somewhere. The moon is a hard bright nickel in the sky.

The mothers begin to speak. Their voices ring in the chill air.

How are you?

Are they ready?

She couldn't sleep last night.

So excited.

How many granola bars did you bring?

Did you bring raincoats?

• • •

The night is silvery with mist. A couple of mothers walk toward you, smiling. Their footsteps crunch on the asphalt. It is not a new sound, though every sound now feels violent against the air. One mother wears a red velour sweatshirt. Another wears a puffy jacket and is rubbing her hands together in the cold. They walk through the world as though it is still the world. Their innocence is a sort of violence and makes you want to look away. Their feet touch the ground; their faces become visible as they get closer. You look at them in disbelief. Then they are standing beside you.

Is she excited for the trip?

I didn't know what to pack.

Do you think they'll be cold?

I packed extra socks so they won't be cold.

Do you think they'll sleep? I don't think I'll sleep!

We can ask the teacher to make them call us.

Do you think they have Benadryl in the first-aid kit? I brought Benadryl for the first-aid kit.

They stand in the darkness, their children climbing onto the bus. The mothers are afraid, but for the wrong thing. Everyone stands together. You see their breath flash, white, into the air. You see one unzip her child's backpack to check that the water bottle is inside. You see another rummage through her purse to find one more granola bar. You watch them talk, waiting for a sign that will tell you why they did what they did. You watch their hands, the way they cut through space carelessly, you hear them laugh. You listen to their laughter; it seems like it is coming from far away, from another nation. But, still, they laugh. You watch their eyes and their faces and they are just eyes and faces.

They resemble the mothers they had been, and laugh and touch one another gently on the arm, and they voted for him.

They look exactly the same.

That is why you cannot forgive them.

Mrs. America

The election was close and she wanted to win, she wanted to win, and now, in the limo, there was the green scent of the campaign advisors' aftershave—the sultry, ruined odor of gangsters—and now, also the sour odor of fear. The TV screen, the bright square, droning constantly, in the black vinyl seat. The men, only men, taking the constant pulse of her popularity—shouting out, at random moments, the progress: "Two points up in Bladen County!" or "Spike in New Brunswick!" The win seemed a distant, abstract goal, but they all agreed they could reach it, and that her win of the seat in

North Carolina would allow their party to take control of the Senate, the nation. They all agreed: this was good. The limo was where she lived now, more than anywhere, as she was driven from one church or banquet hall or multipurpose room to another, where she stepped out of the dim car to the sunlight, and to sudden, shocking applause.

She had never ridden in a limo before this but she was becoming accustomed to it, the unnaturally silent ride over the highways, the sounds of everyday life existing in a distant realm—they were not necessary here. The constant driving, the frantic, unknown schedules, elicited in her a sensation—not passivity, which was not her state, but more a sense that her future did not belong to her. The consultants claimed to understand everything about her appeal, and for months now, since they decided that the people were calling for her, they wanted someone like her to represent them. She stood in front of church groups and told audiences that she had been called to this, that Jesus had called her to this role, which felt special enough; but more, she loved the fact that the campaign staff had confirmed her glorious suspicion: that she was destined to be a senator, that someone had seen something significant in her.

There was one person in the way of her triumph. Mr. Massoud, the thin-shouldered accountant, a state senator from Cary—a man whose parents came here from Beirut, who had caramel skin and black hair. Somehow, he was drawing larger crowds than she was now.

"He's ahead," said Peyton, the gloomy number cruncher from DC, who always gave the impression of being damp.

"Two points in Chapel Hill, five around Asheville. Three in Durham. He could win."

"Neck and neck in New Hanover County," said Harris, a wriggly man who never seemed to wear a seatbelt and was usually shuffling wildly through thick, mysterious files, looking for answers. "What can we throw at him? Affairs, money-laundering, what?"

They gazed at the photo on their phones—Mr. Massoud, his arms stretched around his wife, two daughters, and a son.

He was thin, the sharp thinness of someone who strained, constantly, toward dreary logic. She had been surprised when she met him in person, his skin darker than in his campaign photos, which had apparently been doctored so that he appeared lighter. He did not have the dizzyingly bright smiles of the white Southern men who usually ran for these positions, but a more contained expression, not a smile, which unnerved her—where was the smile? What did people think when he did not smile?—but a set gaze into the horizon, as though he believed that he was supposed to win.

"Would you trust this guy flying a plane?" said Harris, gleefully. "No. Not in Bladen County. So would you trust him with our government?"

"Keep going."

"Where was he born? Beirut?"

"No, Raleigh. His parents had a restaurant there."

They sat around, disappointed.

"I was in Beirut once," said Harris, who sometimes seemed wistful. "A conference. Great beaches—"

"Why the hell would they move from Beirut to Raleigh?"

"He's going to announce a fatwa."

"The guy's not Muslim. He belongs to First Presbyterian. His father went on missions back to the Middle East."

"Jesus."

"Isn't helping us in this case."

"Help us out, Mrs. America," said Harris. "Remember what he said. At the debates. Backstage."

She was, they said, America. She watched the television commercial they broadcast about her, which showed her walking through a pine forest, hands thrust into the pockets of a denim jacket, her face turned up to the light filtering through the trees' long arms. The editing made her appear to be a great leader. It confirmed a private idea she had about herself, a sense of her immense goodness. Finally, others understood it too. Other times, she stared at the ad, shocked to see herself wandering through the forest, and wondered if she won if she would feel like the woman in the advertisement. If she won, she wondered if she would be freed, lifted off the bruised surface of human life, if she would herself be somehow godlike, if she would be able to walk on air.

Now as she was driven through the state, she got texts from the advisors, texts from her mother, and texts from the children. Now ages seventeen, thirteen, ten, eight. *How did she raise four children while doing all of this? And seeming so down-to-earth?* People asked her. How.

"Casseroles!" was what they told her to say. The crowd always laughed. But she was aware of the dragon dankness in their breath. How did she stand up on that stage in those tailored shirts, how did she manage to climb out of the fear and drudgery that boxed them all in? Because she did. There was the thrill of triumph as she stood over them, their damp fingers gripping the stage as though they were holding on to the edge of a ship.

She could (if she was that sort of person) step on them.

How.

She did not tell the audience about the "how"—they could not know how she resembled them. She did not tell them about the mornings inside the rental they moved to after the office supply business failed, after they had gone bankrupt. The smell in the kitchen of Pop-Tarts, of fear. Her mother, after her father left, moved into Carol's house, mourning her old life, yes, at first unable to pour her own coffee or make her bed; her son Adam, then five, born with Down's and nick-named Angel, bringing bags of Skittles to school to hand to the other students so they would not run away from him; her daughter, Mary Grace, thirteen, running out the door in crop tops, already in a race with her friends to reveal the most skin, Harrison and Eli engineering physical battles over the mere fact that the other existed. Carol microwaved rubbery waffles for them and fled. Carol headed out to her job as a manager at Home Depot, working for the same company that destroyed them, her husband, Ted, waking up in the morning, making the calls that weren't answered, and turning for solace to local

paintball leagues, large men, former military, who darted behind large vinyl beanbags clutching plastic armament, shooting paint at each other, shouting, and then staggering off the
dusty field, exhausted by the fact that they had stumbled off
the fake battlefield alive.

The limo floated past gray fields that grew sweet potatoes,
towns scattered around Walmarts, the boxy outlet stores near
Wilson, the broken barns on worn-out farms, the furry green
stands of pine, blue mist in the mountains.

When she looked out the window, she sometimes thought
of how she had risen to this new stature. It began three years
ago—sitting in Adam's kindergarten, where the children
shunned him, and he asked a child to pray with him, and the
teacher smiled and said, "No prayer allowed here." That was
what she said. Carol got a bike lock from her car and chained
herself to the school fence, declaring she would remain there
until prayer was permitted. She made the local news and
rose on the tide of that to City Council, to county commissioner; the meetings became crowded as citizens, both for and
against, came to voice their concerns. She wanted to stomp on
them all, to crush them flat with her foot, and thus she wanted
this: she wanted prayer in schools and marriage only between
a man and a woman and life for unborn babies. She loved listening to her voice when she made these proclamations, and
the arguments involving God were a relief, truly, for she did
not have to remember facts. No one could argue with God.

So she stood onstage, in the suits they bought for her—for the fund-raisers, the dinners in dark rooms with low-lit chandeliers, the nice donors. She shook so many hands. The suits were composed of a material she had never worn before, a silk blend that was so smooth it seemed she was wearing sheets of light.

During the debates, she sometimes looked at Mr. Massoud across the stage and wondered what he, too, was not saying about his family. Mr. Massoud spoke of his father and his waking up at five a.m. to prepare food for his restaurant, the Southern Oasis, in Raleigh. He spoke of the public universities that he attended. He said *he* was America.

But the women whose hands she grasped, the women who rushed to the podium after she spoke—they thought *she* was America. There was a tide of them now, lining up—busloads of housewives from Pender, from Bladen County. The campaign organized the buses, ordered cupcakes from Walmart, which she never ate, but the voters did. Cupcakes iced with the letter *C*. The women all resembled her own mother, and smelled like her—hands with the odor of cookie dough hand sanitizer. She wiped her own hands off with Purell thoroughly after.

Carol did not tell them that three years ago, her father had driven off with one suitcase, two of his best suits, and the coffeemaker. He sent a postcard that he was happy working at a car dealership in Thousand Oaks, and had found his true love with a junior assistant there.

After her father drove off, finally, her mother collapsed. One afternoon, Carol came by her house and found her in the dark. Her mother was sitting on the floor of her bedroom. In her stillness, the position of her legs, she looked like an enormous doll. Her mother's unhappiness was like a coffin sealing them in. "Stand up," Carol said. She touched her mother's arm; she could feel the allure of that failure, the desire to crawl into her mother's clothes; she had a premonition of her own death, of absolute failure inside her cells. She could not bear this. She could not. This was how she would ensure her difference from that: she would win.

Carol sat in the backseat of the limo, skimming facts the campaign managers thought she should know. Her managers kept close track of her schedule, and she was not always aware of where they were taking her. The campaign scheduled a stop at a local mall. As the limo slowed, she looked out the tinted windows to see the entrance of the mall, and saw her daughter with some other teenagers. They stood at the curb by a wrinkled, dull Honda. They were large as horses, and their hair was as bright as Easter eggs—one girl's hair was dyed magenta and another had hair that was turquoise blue. One of the boys had a ring in his nose like a bull. She saw the boy/bull put his hand on Mary Grace's shoulder. They were about to get into the car.

"Hold on," she told the driver.

Carol set down the file she was studying—polls that affirmed voters' desire for her to be tough on crime and to support unregulated gun ownership—and stepped out of the car. She hesitated and walked, crisply, in her gleaming fund-raiser pumps, to the group of young people on the sidewalk. Mary Grace's face reddened. Carol was not sure how to approach them now, as a candidate for national office, so she held out her hand.

"I'm Mary Grace's mother." She paused and added, "I'm running for Senate."

The group froze.

"Hello, ma'am," said the boy who resembled the bull.

"Let's go!" said Mary Grace.

They were staring at her, and not with awe.

"Where are you going?" asked Carol.

"To a movie," said one, and the others softly laughed.

"A movie of me," the one with the turquoise hair said, in a somewhat chilling way.

"Can we just *go*," said Mary Grace.

The bull-boy took a small step toward her. "Mrs. Forrest," said the bull-boy, crossing his arms demurely, but looking pained. "I don't want to pray in school."

"Jackson, like you do anything in school," a girl crowed.

"Not to no one," he said, and, horrifyingly, winked at her.

The boy slipped into the car with the others and it zoomed away. Carol watched it turn the corner. Why had her daughter looked at her as though she were an ant? Why were the teenagers so tall? The inside of her palms felt like ice. She had the sense that the car was running over her, crushing her bones, even as it was simply heading out of the parking lot. She wanted to duck back into the limo, for she just wanted to sit there, in darkness, but she sensed some of the other shoppers staring at it. They recognized her, expecting a smile. Expecting her. Peyton stood beside her, holding a clipboard.

"What was *that*?" asked Peyton.

"Children," she said.

When Carol returned home from the trail, she knocked on the door of her daughter's room. The door was always locked. She stood for a few minutes, waiting for the girl to answer. It felt like begging. Whenever Carol asked her anything, her daughter took it as an affront. Even if Carol asked in a nice way. Who were these friends? What was she doing in her room? Why did that boy have a ring in his nose? The questions were like a drill sliding off a smooth slab of granite. She could always detect the girl's infant face lurking inside her current features, which seemed a terrible, relentless joke.

Mary Grace was skilled at not answering questions, was deft at running out of the house when Carol pressed her, saying, *Fine. Later.* The debates became sharp, sometimes, Massoud's voice ringing through the auditoriums, restating her comments in ways that were wrong, *wrong*, but she never trembled when she debated him. Gripping the lectern in an auditorium, she never trembled as she did when Mary Grace looked at her with her large blue eyes and ran away from her.

• • •

A few days later, there was a text from her mother:

Trouble with Mary Grace. Come home.

Carol grabbed hold of the door handle of the limo and yanked it.

"What are you doing?" asked Harris.

"Something happened," she said.

"Two hundred women, eager to *donate*, are at the Women of Fayetteville luncheon . . ." Peyton quickly sat up.

She was a desired commodity now, which meant that for a brief moment, she had power.

"I'll go back later. Drive me home."

They dropped her off at her home, which was still standing, walls, shrubbery intact. Her daughter was walking quickly, breathless, behind Carol's mother. She wanted something. What was her mother going to show her? A knife? No. A condom? No. A phone. Mary Grace behind her, face red, trying to grab it back.

"What is going—" Carol started.

"God have mercy," said her mother.

She pressed Mary Grace's phone into Carol's hand. There was her daughter's Twitter feed.

Will anyone talk to me? #boredoutmymind #lonelygirl

"Read the next," said her mother.

After the shower #nakedcutie #it'scometothis #givemea towelordon't

There was her daughter, gleaming from the shower. There

were her daughter's breasts, round, the nipples, gleaming from the shower. Not her face; she had cropped that out.

Three hundred retweets, 789 likes.

Carol's throat tightened, as though she were drowning.

"Jackson said it was cute so I said he could retweet me."

The phone radiated heat in her palm.

"Help!" Carol yelled. Fingers shaking, she deleted the tweet, the account. The Twitter handle was @MG2587, which sounded, she hoped, like anyone. She hoped the breasts could not be traced to Mary Grace. Was the offending tweet gone now? Where was it? She stood, pressing keys on the phone, trying to think.

"I'm popular!" said Mary Grace, astonishingly upbeat. "Three hundred retweets!"

Carol stared at her. "What?" she asked.

Mary Grace shrugged.

"You care about how many votes," she said.

"That is *different*," she said. "That is for the future of the United States." She paused. "Who told you to do this?"

"A lot of people do it." She paused. "Give me my phone."

"No," Carol said.

"It's my phone!"

"Nope, mine now." She gripped the phone; it made a soft, living sound in her palm, like a cow.

"I need it! People know me now—"

"Know you? As what? What about your reputation? Your future, Mary Grace? Do you think about that?"

Mary Grace was staring at her, unblinking.

"Do you ever think of *me*?" Carol asked.

"Your future isn't *mine*," said Mary Grace, crisply. "*You* made us move and you made me go to this stupid-ass school—"

"It wasn't me—"

"Where everyone knows each other and now—" Mary Grace stood, lifting her chin, trembling. "Now they know *me*," said Mary Grace, and ran out the front door.

Carol rushed out to follow her. The street was empty. The limo was gone. Mary Grace was running. Carol wanted to call after her, but she did not want her neighbors to hear her sad, hoarse voice in the air. Her throat burned. The lawn was brittle, dying under her feet.

She texted Ted.

Hi hon. MG tweeted naked photos of her body. 300 people retweeted.

There was no response for seventeen minutes, then

Is this a joke?

No. I deleted them!

Ur joking.

Ted. Its under control

Shit.

They're gone. I think. I pressd delet. I took her phone away

Where r they now

Idk

Did you delet

I deleted and deleted

lll smack her ass.

Wait. I'm in a campaign.

The phone was silent for a few minutes.

Nothing happened he texted.

What?

She didnt tweet it stop.

Ted?

Stop making this crap up shes good

What

Stop it stop it stop

Her head hurt. Perhaps he was right. It was not true! There were no naked tweeted photos! But she had seen them. She had seen those breasts on that tiny screen. Now perhaps thousands had seen her child's breasts. What did this do to a person? A candidate? The mere thought of these strangers looking at Mary Grace in this way made Carol feel as though she could feel the cold through her shoes on the sidewalk.

Ted

Ted

She gripped the phone, her hand trembling, and called him. But he had turned off his phone.

In the limo that afternoon, she watched the cars through the dark glass. She often wondered who was inside of them, where they were going, and also, of course, what the drivers and passengers thought of her. But now, as the limo passed them, she had a new impulse—to duck. Someone was going to attack her. This idea was so clear and logical it was as though she recognized herself in a mirror. Someone was going to attack her. She was not afraid when she had this idea; instead, she felt, oddly, a pure and comforting relief. Her fear, somehow, made her safe. Her fear felt logical—it soothed her. She was afraid of the others in the cars around her, the others whom she could not see. Some drivers in these cars would roll down the windows and start shooting at her, some of them would kidnap her children, some of them would sleep with her husband; her mouth was dry as the limo shot into the light draining from the world.

She did not tell the advisors about the naked tweets. She tapped her phone, searching for them on the netherworlds of the Internet, tried to find them on Twitter, but they had fled to some other unreachable realm. If she searched under #nakedshower (shielding her phone carefully with her hand, obviously, so the advisors wouldn't see), there were numerous other teens, an astonishing number, but not, thank god, Mary Grace. She saw the expanse of naked teens and she began to shake, the sheer volume of nakedness and the hands grabbing and retweeting, as though they were touching Mary Grace, they were pushing Angel away from them on the playground, they were the world grabbing at her children, grabbing at her, throwing all of them away.

The advisors, for all their constant phone gazing, didn't know. Their ignorance was both a relief and somehow troubling. Carol waited for the advisors to know, for this journey to end. The road stretched on, flat, to nowhere, to shame that was more terrifying than death. She wanted to win, she wanted to win.

She turned off her phone.

Peyton looked at her.

"Massoud's ahead in your county," he said. "Help us."

She closed her eyes.

"He said he sleeps with dogs," Carol said.

He had said this at a debate, a light, offhand comment. "In our house, we sleep with our dog." What question had he been responding to? He had probably been advised to say something personal, light, to be warmer. She knew what he had really meant—that the dog slept at the foot of his bed. Or even in his bed, as theirs did.

She saw them look at each other.

"I don't know," said Harris, rubbing his large bald head, "will they get it?"

"It's true," she said, sitting up, and finally, she thought, this would win it. She wanted to slap them, finally, to rouse them to action, whatever it took, for this felt correct, and they were looking at her, the aides, with, she thought, a new and deeper respect.

"It'll work," Peyton said.

The crowds at her feet, the lights in her eyes, the roar of the cheering.

• • •

A photo that Ted texted to the family: his team, atop a manu-factured hill, guns lifted, all shouting. They were in a field in Jacksonville. They had won something.

What?

Second place Statewide Tournament!

Why not first?

He did not answer this text. She was just asking.

Ted came home tired from the tournament the next day. He held his gun tenderly. His arm was covered in red welts.

"What happened?" she asked, touching it; he flinched.

"Surprise attack," he said. "Didn't see them coming."

"Who," she said.

He looked away.

The rest of his skin was paler, dim. He stood up, stretched, and she could not look at the welts, red and raised. Why had he not been able to move faster? She was engulfed by a deep embarrassment by that, by her own slide toward age, by the sense they were hurtling, with great speed, toward nothing.

"Don't worry, hon," she said, trying to sound upbeat, "I'm going to win."

The advisors were eager for her to bring up the comment about the dogs. Get it into the airspace! Now! She was attending an-other luncheon. She watched him, Mr. Massoud, during the Q and A. He was on target that day, leaning into those facts, the crowd cheering his responses more than hers; she heard the roar of applause, for him. That enthusiasm washed over her, a chill tide. The TV camera lights made the room look hazy, not quite real.

"Character is important in a candidate for Senate. What do you think of your opponent's moral character?"

"Oh, Mr. Massoud. I wish him well. Certainly we don't agree on many issues. Though I did hear," she said. She blinked and peered into the camera's starlight. "I did hear that he sleeps with his dog."

Some light laughter. She paused.

"I couldn't quite believe it. He said he, well, sleeps with his dog," she said again, and this time she added the slight outraged emphasis on *sleep* so that they would know that she did not, in fact, mean sleep. This time the laughter lifted, hesitantly, then stopped.

"No more questions!" said Harris, clapping. "Let's hear it for Carol. Our next senator in the great state of North Carolina."

He grasped her by the elbow. "Beautiful," he whispered. Inside the limo, there were high fives. She said he slept with dogs. Her eyelids felt like rubber; she blinked. This was what he had said. She had thought nothing when he first said it. But she found herself open to the suspicion she had introduced. This would work. Why could it not be true? She heard their laughter; they had all agreed on something. She craved that agreement, that affirmation that she and the audience were alike. She felt that a part unknown to her had been liberated. She wanted to weep with relief at escaping an unnamed prison.

She would never, like her mother, sit alone in the darkness. She would stride through the world and feel the bushes crunch under her feet.

In the limo, they monitored the news. The regional news outlets picked up her comments with glee, running the video of her saying it that night. The national news grabbed it, too, running it on TV and online. She was trending on Twitter, with different hashtags: #conservativelies, #tellitlikeitis, #whatdoesCarolsleepwith, #fansofCarol, #thedogsvote, #Carolisabitch, #Forrest2016. She had become a ghost, a joke; she could not keep track of the comments about her, the terrible cartoons that equated her with a dog, the memes that made her so ugly, but she was all anyone was talking about, and she hovered over the nation like something else—a cloud.

Then she was home.

When Carol walked into her house, she wondered if her presence on national television would make her family treat her in a new way. She stepped into the living room and waited. No one came to greet her. She opened the door to see her mother hunched in front of the television, the cool light blazing on her face. Her mother did not even notice Carol in the room; she was entranced, staring at the TV, watching her there instead.

Carol waited. "Hello," she said.

"Here you are," her mother said, blinking.

Then Carol saw her daughter coming toward her. Her

blonde hair now cut short, in a wedge shape, a platinum color found nowhere on earth but on furious young people's heads.

"What happened to your hair?"

"Tanya helped me. Isn't it cool?"

Carol reached forward to touch it; Mary Grace stood still. Her hair was dry, the consistency of a broom.

"You ruined your hair," said Carol.

Mary Grace recoiled. "Why don't you just say it looks nice!" she said.

"I'm telling you the truth," said Carol, crisply.

"Well," said Mary Grace. "How nice." Her gaze was sharp, as though she was trying to locate something under Carol's skin. "I heard what you said about that man," she said.

"We are in a campaign," said Carol.

"Jackson said what you said about that guy was stupid," said Mary Grace, haughtily. "Sick."

Mary Grace stood, very still, balancing on a piece of ice.

"Jackson?" Carol said slowly. "With the ring in his nose? The one who didn't want to pray?"

"He's in my bio class," said Mary Grace.

Carol was afraid of her daughter's stare. "I am on national television," said Carol.

When her daughter looked at her, her face was heavy. "I know," she said.

What did Mary Grace know? Did she know of Carol's troubled dreams, in which Jesus kissed her, a real kiss, as though they were married, and she woke up wanting more? Did she know of the times she texted Ted and it seemed he had vanished into the air? Did she know how some nights Carol could not sleep, wishing she could hold her children, and sometimes they did not enter her mind at all? Or did she know the dream in which Carol was lying on a highway, unable to scream, as a truck carrying baskets of lemons rolled over her with its enormous tires, crushing every bone? What did she know? This comment stuck in her mind as the limo floated across the state. The team picked Carol up the next morning, the inside of the limo sugary and warm with the scent of cinnamon buns. The advisors erupted into shouts as the advisors looked at the polling results. "They love you in Duplin County. Damn, they love you in Durham, no shit!"

That was the power of excitement—it sealed you in. Carol thought about what her daughter had said. Usually this thought fluttered outside of the limo, a distant, troublesome idea. Sometimes she recalled her daughter's bright, hard gaze. It was as if her daughter disliked the very sight of her, and understood something about her that was not good. When Carol had this thought, her skin started to burn. It was a low, crackling burning, right beneath the surface, and she wanted it to go away. She feared it might grow, it might consume her—she wanted it to stop.

What made the burning stop was this: the advisors' joyful cries when the polls went up. The excitement was better; it was solid, it was a grand, windowless mansion with silver walls; it made them all light and airy and they could fly and it sealed everything else out. She stared at the charts on the phones. Forrest: 49 percent, Massoud: 47 percent, 4 percent undecided. Forrest: 50 percent, Massoud: 48 percent, 2 percent undecided.

At the next debate, Mr. Massoud approached her before they went onstage. They usually shook hands at the beginning of the debate and said something disparaging about the junk food backstage. This time he walked past the snack table, past the advisors, right to her.

"Carol," he said. He usually called her "County Commissioner Forrest"—which felt both courteous and demeaning. He looked particularly trim that evening, clad in a new navy suit, his glossy black hair parted on the side; he looked a bit handsome, a perception that she found alarming.

"Retract the lie," he asked.

He was standing very straight, his arms crossed against his chest, looking at her with a cool paternal gaze; she resented that.

"You did say you slept with your dog," she said.

"You let them believe this meant something else." He stepped back. "Do you even understand what you said, Ms. Forrest?"

"Don't speak to me that way," she said.

"A boy threw a can at my daughter when she was walking to school," he said. "He barked at her."

She saw, in the violet shadows under his eyes, that he had

not been sleeping. She had spent many nights not sleeping either, she thought. The same thing happened to her son, she wanted to tell him, for a different reason.

"What would you say to my child, Carol?" he asked, his voice steelier. "After the lie you told about her father?"

She looked away from him, at the chairs for the audience.

"I would tell her she is not a dog," she said.

That night when she opened the door, she heard Ted and Mary Grace talking in the living room. Mary Grace was laughing, a sound she had not heard in some time. Ted looked up when Carol walked in. Mary Grace was clutching something; her fingers closed over it. A phone.

"She needed a new phone," he said. "One of my buddies on the team gave it to me cheap—"

Carol watched Mary Grace gaze lovingly at the screen.

"Come here," Carol said, gesturing to Ted. They went into the kitchen.

"What did you do?" she whispered.

"I can't see my girl crying—"

"For god's sake. She tweeted naked photos. Of herself."

His face twitched. "Stop it," he said. "Where are they? Show me."

She looked at her own phone; she did not know where to begin searching for the pictures.

"They were here," she said, frightened. "They were here—"

"I don't see them," he whispered.

She stared at him. His eyes were like a baby's, glazed and blue.

"Daddy," Mary Grace called from the other room, "thank you."

Ted nodded; he looked happy to be appreciated.

"You're welcome," he said, staring right at Carol.

With all the campaigning, she and Ted had not slept together in some weeks, and that night, he wanted to. She was mad because of the phone, but went along. There was the weight of his body on hers, and he felt heavier, from being fired upon or muscle or sadness, and he held her buttocks and moved into her swiftly, hard, as though he were trying to win an argument with someone else. Suddenly, she thought of Mr. Massoud, the way he gripped the lectern and spoke to the audience, to her, and she felt, with shame, that Mr. Massoud knew her better than anyone, that he listened to her more closely and with more respect, and she wanted to be up there again, speaking to him, convincing the audience that she was America. She closed her eyes but there was Mr. Massoud's face, still, looking at her with his dark eyes, waiting for her to rebuff his statement, and she cried out, for she did not know what to say to him, how to answer anyone, as her husband rolled off her, while, in her own room, asleep, Mary Grace clutched the phone to her chest.

• • •

The next debate was at the Hilton in Raleigh. When she arrived, the crew in the limo grew quiet at what they saw; five television vans, from stations local and far away, and a fresh tide of reporters breaking over the sidewalk as the limo approached. They were here for the candidates, for Mr. Massoud and for her.

"Showtime," said Peyton, helping her out.

There was the liberal media, rushing forward, her advisors holding out arms to block them, trim young women who lunged at her with microphones and asked: What did you mean? Are you exploiting Americans' fear of citizens from the Middle East to win? Why did you let North Carolina voters believe he was engaging in bestiality?

"Ms. Forrest didn't say it, Mr. Massoud did," called one of her advisors to the reporters.

The advisors guided her inside and gasped. The room was packed with people waiting for them, the bitter scent of close bodies in the air.

She and Mr. Massoud took their places at their lecterns. When she shook hands with him before they started, he gripped her hand even more firmly than usual, and she could feel his heartbeat in his palm, and then he released it quickly, as though he could not bear to touch her.

She saw the taut faces of some of the audience; the air in the room was hot.

First question: How would they create jobs in the state? Mr. Massoud first. But when he spoke, a couple of men near the front interrupted him.

"Answer this!" they called. "Do you sleep with dogs?"

Mr. Massoud held up his palm as he often did when people asked him aggrieved questions, as though patting their heads. His forehead was damp. "Do you have pets?" he asked. "We do. A collie named Fluffy. Our daughter named her. She sleeps at the foot of our bed. Would you like to see a picture?" He held up a Christmas photo of his family surrounding a golden collie. Each of them wore a red bow affixed to their outfit; the collie had one on his collar. Some audience members applauded, heartily, as though this photo told them everything they needed to know.

Carol stared. Why had her campaign not thought of this? Would anyone in her family but Angel have willingly worn a bow? She did not have a photo available.

Mr. Massoud asked, "Ms. Forrest. Do you have any photos of your family you would like to share?"

It was a brilliant move. Why would she have a photo on her? Did he know? Did his campaign know about Mary Grace?

He had the innocent face of an accountant, blank as a lake.

"Not with me," she said. "But don't mess with me, Mr. Massoud." She heard her prim, outraged voice ring throughout the room, a voice she conjured simply for the debates. "I know who you are."

A roar swelled from the crowd, a confused half laugh, half shout. It was so loud she felt the laughter shuddering in her feet. What was the sound coming from the crowd? Was it agreement, appreciation, would it make her win? There was applause, the sound was more than a laugh—it seemed like it arose from a howling animal. She noticed a couple of men moving toward the stage. The expression on their faces was reptilian and intent. She smiled at the audience and then one of the men barked and threw an object. It flew over the stage and hit Mr. Massoud.

Glass shattered; it was a bottle. He shouted and fell down; she saw he was bleeding.

The actions in the room changed. There was no more debate. There were policemen, shouting and rushing toward Mr. Massoud, and two hurling themselves off the stage into the audience. The people in the crowd boiling, a couple of men turning to hit one another. Mr. Massoud's wife, clad in a cream-colored suit, ran up to the stage and knelt by him; there were stains of blood on her suit. She had seen Mrs. Massoud backstage an hour ago in that suit, carefully eating a potato chip so as not to get crumbs on it.

"Jesus fucking Christ," she heard Peyton say, sharply, and then someone said, "Get her out of here." The doors of the hotel flung open, and she was walking, guided by Peyton and a police officer, outside, and she was being put inside the limo, the vinyl cool behind her back, and the car was driving off.

"Where are we going?" she asked.

She was alone in the limo. It pulled away from the Hilton. Where were Harris, Peyton, the rest? The driver was talking to his radio. "Heading to I-40."

"What is happening?" she asked.

"They said to drive you out of there," said the driver. He paused. "What happened?"

"Nothing," she said.

It was strangely easy to say this.

"Lots of police," said the driver.

"There was a bottle," she said. Did someone actually throw it at him? Did it slip out of someone's hand?

"What happened?"

She paused. "Mr. Massoud had a bottle land on him."

The driver coughed. "It landed on him?"

"Yes."

She met his eyes in the rearview mirror and looked away.

"Well, damn," he said. "How'd it *land* on him?"

"I don't know," she said.

Her cell phone buzzed. It was Mary Grace. She answered it. She heard a deep, shuddering sigh.

The limo passed other hotels, a mall with a Bed Bath & Beyond, a Costco, parking lots. Carol believed she had passed this scenery on the campaign trail, but she wasn't sure. There was the flat sound of nothing inside the limo, she heard nothing, and she was supposed to be hearing applause, but instead there was just the rush of the wheels against the earth.

"I saw the debate," said Mary Grace, softly.

She was, for a moment, flattered. "You did! What did you think—"

"I heard what you said."

Mary Grace's voice was husky. Carol was confused; she realized that Mary Grace had been crying.

"I simply repeated his own words—" said Carol.

"Stop running," said her daughter, firmly. "Now."

The way she said it, Carol thought she meant running from what? "No," Carol said. "I will never drop out. I don't want—"

She listened to Mary Grace's breath; she was still crying.

"Mary Grace?" Carol asked.

"Look at Twitter," said Mary Grace.

"What do you mean?" asked Carol, alarmed. "What?"

"Look at it. Now." Mary Grace hung up.

The world was melting and Carol did not know how to stop it.

She clicked on Twitter. What should she search for? She scanned the search feed and saw a column: Trending. There was #ForrestMassoudDebate and #CutDowntheForrest and #Dogfest and #MaryGracePhotos. She saw a name retweeted, @CarolForrest'sDaughter, and there was her daughter, naked, and there was her face.

In the moment that Carol stared at her phone, trying to push the buttons that would erase this, everything, but would not, before she saw the Twitter account that held the naked pictures of Mary Grace, sent all over the world, before Carol heard her cell phone begin to buzz, over and over, before she felt herself begin to fall, she thought this: that the advisors in the limo were the ones who had understood her most of all, that in all of the long days inside that car with them, the constant low, sourness of their breath, they had known everything about her, and they had believed in this simple fact—that she could save their country, that Mrs. America was good. She could not explain to her daughter that America needed her, Carol Forrest. It was the thought that calmed her when she could not ask her husband to come home, when she could not comfort her son, when she had come upon her mother weeping in the dark, when she did not know what to say to her daughter. She sat in the limo, alone, looking out the tinted windows, at the stands of pine. She did not know how to convince her daughter this was the only thing that was true in this world, that this was the one fact she understood—that the advisors and the voters in the audience were correct, that she was Mrs. America, and that she, Carol Forrest, was not like everyone else.

This Is Who You Are

My preferred seat in Hebrew school was by the window, and when I was restless, which was often, I looked outside. There were the Santa Monica Mountains, gauzy with chaparral, sloping down to the basketball court like an enormous, wrinkled rug. Once, I saw a coyote trot down the mountain. Another time I watched the way a blue shadow from a eucalyptus tree stretched slowly across the brown lawn. As the afternoon wore on, I sometimes tried to imagine what it would be like to be something out there: the coyote, the shadow, the mountain. But that afternoon I only saw Ava, the temple secretary, running from the front office, hurrying toward our classroom, toward us.

The sight of Ava moving at all was startling—Ava was usually seated, like a statue, at the front desk of Temple Shalom, and no one ever saw her run. She was a solid woman around sixty, with one arthritic foot, and she hurtled unevenly down the concrete path from the temple to the classrooms. When she stumbled in, breathing hard, she regarded us with a new and wary expression, as though we were all made of ice and about to melt. Then she whispered something to our teacher, Darlene, who looked at her and then us and said, sharply, "School is dismissed."

We had been practicing the V'ahavta, which Darlene, a student of Judaic studies at UCLA, taught by timing it, meaning that she went around the room with a stopwatch while we tumbled through the ancient words of the prayer. Aaron Hochman read it in fifty-seven seconds. Marjorie Silver read it in sixty-six. I was waiting for my turn, for I had practiced and could let that prayer rip off my tongue within fifty.

When class was dismissed, cheers flowered through the room. It sounded like the Dodgers had won, though they were not playing that day. Aaron stood up on his seat and leapt off, pumping his fist in the air. We gathered up our backpacks; Ava rushed out of the room. I wondered why Ava was leaving so quickly, and when I identified the sound she made as she left, I knew—she did not want us to see her cry.

Darlene looked at us.

"Stop laughing," Darlene said.

Darlene marched us to the parking lot of Temple Shalom, a large concrete synagogue near the 405 freeway. Seventeen of us made a ragged line, not knowing whether to celebrate or what. It was the middle of May, 1974. The air was lukewarm and still, but the day now felt somehow fragile, a balloon that was about to pop.

Rabbi Golden joined us in the parking lot. I watched his face carefully, for he was pronouncing his words in a slow and measured way. What he said was not what I expected. He told us that there had been a massacre.

He pronounced the word flatly, but we could hear a tiny tremble in his voice.

"Where?"

"Ma'alot," he said.

Where was that? Was it in the Valley?

"In Israel."

That was far away.

"Terrorists slaughtered children in a school."

The rabbi walked back and forth in front of the carpool pickup zone, looking at the scrubby beige hills. We let this news settle on us and then asked,

Why are *we* going home?

Someone called the religious school director at Wilshire Boulevard Temple. They said they hated Jews.

This was, in my opinion, weirdly funny. Someone muttered to a director at another temple that they hated Jews and then *we* were freed from Hebrew school an hour early? We had lucked out. This development was a peculiar mutation of the general discontent floating through the classroom—that our parents forced us to come here, that the sight of Darlene holding up flash cards of *aleph, bet, gimel,* etc., sometimes made our minds disintegrate with boredom; it was why I liked to stare out the window of the classroom, imagining myself as anything else. Class was from four to six, and though we did not really understand the concept of lost time, we sometimes had the palpable sense that two hours of our lives, two shiny and delicious hours, had vanished. Forever. The cloud of resentment was usually turned toward Darlene, who regarded us with a leaden air of disappointment at our focus on that day's snack options as opposed to our role, just thirty years removed from the Holocaust, to protect World Jewry.

We glanced at one another, silent. Jessica Silverman started crying, instantly, authentically, which annoyed us; she was clearly pandering, or worse, she knew, more precisely, what to feel.

The mothers were driving up in their station wagons as though they had all been waiting, engines running, in some alternate parking lot for this precise moment, each rattling noisily over the speed bump.

"We're all fine," said the rabbi, leaning into each car. He looked around. But what did this mean? A distant coyote yowled, a thin wail. There was the dry, sweet smell of desert, of vanilla, in the air. My mother was talking and I heard this: *They threw a grenade at a group of girls in the corner. A grenade blew the girls to shreds.* My mother had been taking my sister to the doctor that afternoon, as my sister had recently developed problems breathing. The doctors put forth various theories on what it could be; asthma, allergies, or something else. My mother recently went to half-time at her job as a guidance counselor at LAUSD to drive my sister to her appointments; she wanted to figure out what was wrong so she could get back to working full-time again. My sister, Diane, was an accomplished ballet dancer who could do fifty fouetté turns at a time, her leg whipping around, like a machine, while she remained perfectly centered; her body had always worked for her.

Now I lay in bed, listening to my sister breathing beside me, listening to the crinkling in her chest. I thought of the girls in Ma'alot going to school that day, thinking it would be just a regular day. I imagined them walking into their classroom, finding their usual seats, putting their lunches in a cubby. I remembered the way the rabbi walked back and forth in the gray lake of the parking lot, scanning the empty sky.

Apart from Hebrew school twice a week, I went to Thomas Jefferson Junior High, a large public school in West Los Angeles. The members of our Hebrew school class were scattered across other schools in Beverly Hills, Encino, Sherman Oaks, Westwood, Culver City; only Aaron and Marjorie attended Thomas Jefferson Junior High, and though we raised a hand to each other in the hallways, we did not seek each other out. We knew each other in the temple classroom, trying to pronounce the prayers, and this seemed too intimate in Jefferson Junior High's hard glaring light.

Jefferson Junior High was a collection of squat, stucco buildings, the low walls lacy with bougainvillea's magenta petals, but when I walked into a classroom, the flat gray fluorescent light made me feel like I was entering a jail. The air was stale with the end of our childhoods.

The day after we were sent home after Ma'alot, I sat down to lunch with the girls in my group: Hannah Stein, Laila Dixon, Jennifer Nakamura, and Audra Jefferson. We had worked on an arduous project of *A Tale of Two Cities* in English, received an A, and that felt, at the time, like a bond. I knew that our lunch discussion would not refer to Ma'alot. The only one who might know about Ma'alot in the group was Hannah, whose parents had been children in Treblinka and whose mother had a purple number tattooed on her arm. Hannah had a mass of red hair that she tied back in a ponytail, and her primary fashion statement involved tubes of lip gloss—root beer, 7-Up, chocolate mint—which she wore on a string around her neck. Her main goal in life appeared to be getting a better grade than me in all subjects. She would want to claim superior ownership over the attack, citing more details, perhaps, making my own knowledge of the attack minor and stupid, so I didn't want to discuss it around her.

Laila Dixon was the tallest, not religious but vaguely Christian. Her parents hailed from the Ivy League Back East, and they had recently gotten divorced. Laila smelled of coconut and, indistinctly, like a woman; she had long pale hair she twisted into formless shapes when she spoke. Her hair seemed to be its own living entity, with great authority, and her behavior somehow directed the opinions of the others. There was the day when she arrived at the table wearing a white puka shell necklace, and then, in a couple of weeks, the others were also wearing white puka shell necklaces, in an action of rare agreement; Laila's power over the group was to present us with solutions for our bewilderment, and our gratitude to her was that we would follow her.

Also in our group was Jennifer Nakamura, whose parents had been in the internment camps, who was second violin in the school orchestra, never quite first, and who never ate the carefully composed seaweed salads and sushi her mother made for her lunch, a sort of impassioned strike that her mother did not see. She sprayed Sun-In in her long, dark hair; we all used Sun-In to adjust the color of our hair, with varying degrees of success.

Audra Jefferson lived in Baldwin Hills and attended the same ballet school my sister did in Culver City; her brown hair was usually organized into a bun, with combs of alternating silk flowers—roses, lilac, lilies—set into her hair. She traveled to school via the PWT busing system. Our school was, even with a third of the students riding buses forty-five minutes every morning, clearly segregated, with most of the black students gathering in the right quadrangle of the cafeteria, the drill team all black and the cheerleaders almost all white. No one asked why this was.

We recognized in ourselves, in our smallness in this huge, raucous cafeteria, the hot desire to win. It also felt as though we had slid through some escape chute and shot past various terrible historic events to land in this cafeteria, with its lacy magnolia bushes and peacock-like birds of paradise flowers. The elephant ferns shone like butter icing.

It was almost the end of the school year. We were dreading the announcements of the Annual Poll in the school yearbook. There were the general categories, which none of us would win, such as "Prettiest" or "Most Resembles Farrah Fawcett" or "Best Laugh" or, hopefully, not "Best Butt." Hannah and I didn't want to win "Best Nose," which unfailingly (and meanly) went to a Jewish student, and I found myself staring in the mirror, examining myself, wondering if I would be singled out for this, which would be a humiliation I did not think I could bear. Jennifer wanted to win "Best Cartwheel," as she had been taking gymnastics and sometimes showed us her cartwheels and round-offs after lunch, but this award invariably went to the cheerleaders. Audra was afraid of getting "Roberta Flack twin," for it embarrassed her to be compared to such sultriness, though we all sometimes murmured, giggling, the lyrics to "Feel Like Makin' Love," lines that seemed to contain a code for something unnameable but held a great and unwieldy hope.

Today, we talked about Coach Matt Huggins, the PE teacher for the seventh grade. He was a tall man of indeterminate age—somewhere on the far side of twenty. He had blond hair parted on the side and very white teeth, and he smiled at anyone, an easy smile that splashed you with light, a smile that made other students feel noticed but made me feel he was aiming it at someone else. His legs were as large as barbecued hams, and had a sinister quality, covered with dark hair. He wore green-tinted aviator glasses, which made him look as if he were about to pilot a plane, and Hawaiian shirts unbuttoned to the middle of his chest. We discussed what Laila described as his immense sexiness, which she presented as a clear and incontrovertible fact. As we walked through the corridors of the junior high, the world was so mutable—Jake Tivoli's face was soft as a rose and then it was covered by a beard, Stephanie Hall's breasts now bubbled out of her tube tops and she possessed a laugh that sounded like a seagull's cry—we wanted a proclamation, a fact where we could find shelter.

"You know it. He is hot," said Laila, expertly, and we all listened to this.

"He made us run the Ironman today," said Jennifer. "I almost seriously died."

"You're a weakling," said Audra, and laughed.

"Perfect day for it. He probably likes seeing us sweaty," said Laila, with the specific, eerie sort of pronouncement that disturbed us and woke us up.

"That's gross, in my opinion," said Audra.

"He is such a total fox," said Jennifer.

"We are not actually using that word," said Hannah, rolling her eyes.

"What word?" asked Jennifer.

"He's foxy," said Laila, huskily, and we all laughed.

Coach Huggins strolled through the cafeteria, waving to students, boys but mostly the girls. The wave varied; a flat hand, a thumbs-up, hey! There was a self-conscious, theatrical element to it; he seemed to be auditioning for the role of the affable coach on a television show. We watched where he would stop, which girl he would sit beside today.

"It's going to be Avery," said Jennifer; she liked predicting this.

He sat beside Avery Solon, who had recently taken up the cause of makeup—mascara, foundation, eye shadow, lip gloss—as though a naked face were an argument she intended to win. This meant extremely enthusiastic application—she wore so much orange foundation her face appeared to be made of clay. He bent toward her like they were continuing an important conversation. We pretended not to look. But we looked—at the way she laughed, leaning into him, an almost professional-seeming laugh emanating from her shoulders, and we saw him stroke her back, his hand like a slow animal, and we watched how Avery moved closer to him until she was sitting on his lap.

Two days later, when we got to Hebrew school, there was a security car in the parking lot. Bel-Air Security. A heavy graying man sat at the wheel, leafing through a copy of *Consumer Reports* and eating a bag of Cheetos. He seemed very engaged in an article about dishwashers. I doubted that he was capable of preventing us from skipping Hebrew school, let alone a barrage of terrorists.

"What's that man doing here?"

"Security," said Darlene.

"Why?"

"Because."

She did not elaborate further. Darlene was often saddened that we were not advertising our bake sale to raise money for Soviet Jewry, or signing up more sponsors for the annual Solidarity March for Israel. We were never raising enough money for the Jews who were in precarious situations; sending money to them felt like a way of paying them off for our own luck. Darlene's goal was to never let us feel too safe. She clipped news stories about Nazi or KKK groups meeting secretly across the United States. She passed the newspaper stories to us and asked, if we saw a gathering like this in our neighborhood, what were *we* going to do about it? Who would we write to? Call? The sky was hot and white over the Santa Monica Mountains. We passed around the articles about anti-Semites while voraciously consuming our powdered donuts or Twinkies.

"We are going to go on to timing the V'ahavta and the Kaddish today," said Darlene, "but first we want to do something to connect with our brothers and sisters in Israel. Look at this."

She turned on the overhead projector and the many faces from the newspaper flashed on the screen. Twenty-two of them.

We looked at the faces of the dead students.

"Now we will say their names."

No one really wanted to say their names, as if they would stick to our tongues and choke us.

Shoshana.

Ilana.

Tamar.

Yaakov.

"Everyone. Pick one student."

I studied the faces. Of course, we'd all tumble toward the prettiest one, or the one with the brightest smile, or the one who would somehow protect us from a fate like theirs.

"You are going to adopt one dead student and write to their parents. We need to support them."

Darlene's voice cracked and we sat up, alert; she covered her eyes with her hand for a moment. We sat in this bare room, empty except for the seventeen plastic-wood desks, Hebrew letters on bright placards on the wall. Now the room was heavy with various types of emotion. For the first time, ever, I thought it would be preferable to memorize a prayer.

"This is who you are," Darlene said, shuffling through papers. "Pick one."

Aaron raised his hand; his fingers trembled.

"Did any of them live?" asked Aaron.

"No. They are all dead."

We were silent, absorbing this.

I stared at the faces and tried to imagine them waiting, alive, in the corner.

My mind felt restless when I tried to think of certain things—my sister breathing at night beside me, Coach Huggins standing on the square green field watching us run by. I often stared at people and wondered what was in their minds, but did not always want to know it.

We all reluctantly chose a student. I picked Ilana because she was smiling in the photo and she looked smart, like she could possibly escape.

"What do we say?"

Darlene wrote on the board: *Dear family of*

We all carefully copied that. But what then?

Darlene regarded us with a cool expression, as though she was troubled by our lack of skills in this region of sympathy. She sighed.

"Write you are so sorry to hear about the loss of X. We share your grief."

We all wrote that.

"Can we say anything about us?" asked John Blum. "I just got on the Y's traveling baseball team."

"I just made the Area D orchestra."

We looked at her, wondering if sharing our personal moments of triumph would be helpful. Darlene rubbed the eraser against her wrist.

"I don't think this is what they want to hear," she said. "It would seem like bragging. Say something that would make them feel we are thinking of them. Say something kind about the child who was killed."

I looked at the photo of Ilana.

"How about—I think your daughter looks very nice and maybe good at math," said Lisa.

Darlene held her chalk in the air. "Almost," she said. She looked out the window, and she, too, seemed not to know what to say.

"How about something like: 'We love you and the state of Israel. We will stand by you.' That could be something they want to hear."

We wrote that down. We wrote our letters, quickly. Everyone wanted to be done with the letters. I stared at Ilana's face. I did not want her to be dead. The fact of her death kept bumping into my mind and sliding off. I folded my letter into an envelope and addressed it, but I had other thoughts about Ilana. I tried to smile at her face encouragingly.

She escaped, I thought. It made me feel better, for a moment, to imagine this. She crawled out from the pile of bodies and slipped out a window to run and get on a plane. The others were still writing their letters as I took another piece of paper. *Dear Ilana*, I wrote. *I hope you were able to get out of the school. You can find me at Thomas Jefferson Junior High School in Los Angeles. My locker is 541. If you come here, you can live with me. I can help you.*

Darlene said she would mail the letters. Express mail, tomorrow.

I didn't know exactly where to mail the second letter, but I put it on the pile, too.

The Hebrew school classrooms at Temple Shalom were located off the main synagogue. There were just twenty-eight students, grades five to eight. We were familiar with each other, as we began this routine as children. Our parents, many of whom grew up in the 1940s and 1950s and spent energy trying to press down any Jewishness in themselves, dropped us off here and sped away. But there was always a longing in my father's voice when he picked me up—"So what did you talk about?"—he wanted to locate something in me that he tried to erase in himself.

It was assumed that, because we were dropped off here two days a week, in some way we were alike. I peered at my classmates, searching for some similarity between us, some of whom shared the wild dark hair that I had, some who did not. History always felt like it was breathing softly behind us, and for an anxious month when I was eleven, I thought that if we went through the wrong door in the synagogue we'd end up in the shtetl or the Warsaw ghetto or running from Crusaders or in a concentration camp. I did not want to open the wrong door.

But here we were. The air was clear and quiet, the scent of licorice lifting off the golden hills. There was a low-level tension between the public school kids and the private school girls who used Hebrew school as a chance to wear the Jordache jeans and platform shoes they were not allowed to wear during their school day. There was the slap of a basketball on asphalt during break and the distinct shouts of Aaron and Jessica bartering Wacky Packs and most of the boys gathering around Jeff's radio listening to the Dodger game. Though we didn't all really know each other, somehow these hours together, week by week, made us think we did.

The small group was a contrast to Jefferson Junior High. There were so many students it seemed that at first the school was filled with a whole new batch of strangers whenever I moved from one class to another. It was California, which meant that most of our parents or grandparents had come here from somewhere else—the Midwest, the East Coast, the South, Mexico, Japan, China.

There were threads of music rising from tape players, as though an anthem from a distinct nation: Elton John, "Bennie and the Jets" and "Don't Let the Sun Go Down on Me"; Kool and the Gang, "Hollywood Swinging"; Joni Mitchell, "Help Me"; Jackson Five, "Dancing Machine." Laila hated Olivia Newton-John but loved Steely Dan. Jennifer loved Elton John and bought purple sunglasses. Audra liked Stevie Wonder and thought Elton John's outfits were idiotic. Inside the classrooms, thirty of us sat in long rows listening to the teachers drone on, trying to press facts about Spanish verbs, geometry, Dickens, and the American Revolution into our heads, and outside, there was the scent of flowers and the buoyancy of music and the glaring sun and also, in the bubbling rush of people in the school, the lurking sense that at any moment someone could yell something at you or grab you and I scanned the faces striding down the hallway, trying to figure out who we all were.

The teachers were nice sometimes or completely crazy. We sat at the lunch table evaluating them.

"Mrs. Murdoch's gray streak looks like a skunk today," said Jennifer.

"It took over half her head yesterday," said Audra. "How does that happen?"

"And she forgot to collect our homework," said Laila. "Third time."

"What do you have in there?" asked Hannah.

It was the question that perked us all up. What grade did you have? It seemed that the sun had stopped right above us in the sky. Grades were important, for they would sort us. We all agreed on this.

"A," said Audra, quickly.

"A-minus, but with an extra credit I'll have an A," said Jennifer, firmly.

I was quiet. I had a B-plus, which meant I wanted this particular conversation to end.

"What?" asked Jennifer, now alert.

"I haven't checked," I said.

"You had a B-minus on that infinitive quiz," said Laila, who had an exhaustive memory for such things.

"Oh," said Audra, who had mastered a kind of regal pity, "so you probably have a B."

"Plus," I snapped, before I could stop myself, "I have at least a B-plus."

Hannah leaned back, smirking a bit; Laila shrugged and majestically twisted her long golden hair. I jumped up and went to my locker, stepping around the students rolling on the lawn like casualties in a war. I had a secret: in my locker, I stored some extra clothes for Ilana. An old sleep shirt and shorts and flip-flops. While I was somewhat embarrassed that I had done this, I was also a little proud, for I wanted to take some, any, action; I felt I was preparing for her arrival. When

I had trouble focusing in class, I imagined her trudging up to the locker, perhaps at night, her clothes smelly from her long trip; I imagined her wandering through the junior high school to my locker, changing her clothes right then, and slipping on the shirt and shorts I had left for her. She would thank me; she would be grateful that someone believed she was not doomed but could get out of that classroom. I saw her letting out a breath when she had the right clothes, turning around in the warm, honeyed silence, trying to decide what to do next.

My house sat amid a cluster of other ranch houses that all sprang up, simultaneously, around 1960. They had the same basic floor plan, and if you shut one eye and squinted, sometimes they all blurred.

At night, after dinner, my family gathered in the den and watched the news. There was the news about Ma'alot and last month the terror attack at Kiryat Shmona, also in northern Israel. There was, right after Ma'alot, the shoot-out downtown with the LAPD and the Symbionese Liberation Army, who had kidnapped Patty Hearst. As we watched, the walls of the house felt thin. "Little Israel," my father said. "All these enemies around it. Not knowing if your bus will blow up or not. Can you imagine living like this?" He stared at the TV, leaning forward. He taught American history at Santa Monica High School, and his classes were growing bigger each semester, the students uninterested in the topic, sometimes taunting him when they were bored, and recently one threw an eraser at his back when he was writing something on the board. He labored under a principal who he believed favored other teachers, giving them more honors classes and classrooms with lights that always turned on. My father tried generosity and being helpful—giving her tins of cookies for Christmas, volunteering to run the College Prep club and the History Buffs club—but nothing made him feel appreciated. "All these countries," he said, "want to exterminate it. But the Israeli people never give up." He liked using the word "exterminate," and mentioned it often. He wanted the Israelis to teach him something.

I practiced my V'ahavta. My parents liked hearing me practice, liked the sound of the words they did not understand.

"*V'ahavata et adonai elochecha,*" I droned. It was oddly calming to say the words, especially in that the meaning was so abstract and actually dull—*You shall love the Lord Your God with all your heart with all your soul and with all your might.* How did anyone even do this and why? I wondered if I loved my family the correct way. I wanted to be good at love and I didn't know if I was.

The campus was aglow; the pointy flamingo flowers, the elephant palms, it was late May. The cafeteria outside, tables parked on the damp concrete, had the musty odor of a swimming pool. I somewhat admired Laila's clarity in her longing for Coach Huggins, even if it unnerved me; I was trying to understand the logic of my own longing, which fell over random boys in my class. They inhabited my dreams for a few weeks, then vanished. I was not clear why I was drawn to one or another. Tom Laughlin barely resembled a boy; he wasn't one of the large muscled types with beards, who seemed as remote and freakish as apes. He was skinny and had large red lips; he could almost have been a girl. His hair was feathered and blond and was much more beautiful than mine. He balanced on a skateboard as though he were standing on ice. He smelled strongly of pot, a sour lawn, a fact I tried to ignore. I sat behind him in algebra and he tipped his chair back so far his hair almost fell onto my papers. I thought of him so fiercely during the day my forehead hurt.

We watched Coach Huggins walking around on lunch patrol. It was a warm day, and many girls were wearing halter tops, some that resembled mere handkerchiefs tied with strings in the back.

"I have to tell you all something," said Laila.

We leaned closer to her.

"I sat on Coach Huggins's lap after gym yesterday," said Laila. "I needed him to sign my late slip. He said, sure, he held his leg out. I sat on it. He signed it and he was staring at me and he said, 'You're beautiful.'"

We all listened to that.

"No, he didn't," said Hannah.

"Yes, he did," said Laila. She sat up and touched her hair, gently, perhaps the same place he had touched it. Was she beautiful? It seemed an important word, a goal that we all were supposed to want. But he had decided this, somehow, walking across the trampled soccer field.

Audra was sitting very still, and then she said softly, "Ick."
I was glad she said that.

"Come on, it's a compliment," said Laila, flipping her hair
so it fell on the left side of her head.

"Are you getting an A in PE then?" asked Hannah.

"Probably. He wants me to come to his office and talk
about extra credit I can do."

Coach Huggins's office was a small room in the gymna-
sium. There was just room for a desk and a bulletin board, and
on the walls were lots of magazine pages ripped out—mostly
photos of young women athletes posing in wet swimsuits or
with a tennis racket, arm stretched into a serve.

"Well, so sorry he likes *me*," said Laila.

It seemed that a glass wall sprung up then between Laila
and the rest of us. There was the point that she had been admired by Coach Huggins, which separated her, and there was
the point that she embraced that fact, which made the glass
thicker. I could see that the others stared through the glass,
wanting also to be admired by him, and I felt a glass box close
around me, for I was afraid of the way his hand traced the girls'
backs, the way they held still as he did so, drawn into quiet,
animal beings. The way that hand somehow transformed the
girl underneath it, so that she became unrecognizable.

I stood up.

"Where are you going?"

I picked up my dessert. "This tastes horrible. I have to
throw it out."

I picked up the paper container of red Jell-O and carried it to the trash can. I walked a path far from Coach Huggins, past some members of the drill team, who were practicing a routine for a football game that night. They moved with urgency and authority, practicing together. When I slipped by them, they all burst into laughter. I peered into a crowd of elephant palms, hoping I would find a girl there, in the blue shade, crouched, watching us.

When my mother dropped me off in the Hebrew school parking lot the following week, the guard was gone.

I listened to my footsteps on the concrete and was aware that, in the absence of the security guard, I was more alert, but I didn't know for what.

"Where'd he go?" I asked Darlene.

"Budget ran out," Darlene said. She had just gotten a perm like Barbra Streisand and her hair resembled a thatched hut. She started erasing the board in short, angry swipes.

"What about the terrorists?"

She paused.

"Things have calmed down," she said, continuing to erase the board.

"How do you know that?"

She looked out the window, at what appeared to be nothing. This alarmed me.

"Did we get a letter back?" I asked.

"No," she said.

"When will we?"

This Is Who You Are

Darlene sighed, sharply.

"I don't know when," she said.

My sister's cough was now such a normal sound in the house that I found myself doing it. My own coughing began one night as a clearing of my throat that I did once, then twice, then every few minutes. It came on like a hammer inside me, pressing against my throat. My mother heard me one morning while I was pouring cornflakes, and she rushed into the kitchen to see if I was choking.

"Are you okay?" she asked.

"I think," I said, recognizing her face of concern, usually turned toward my sister. I coughed again.

"Can you stop?"

I did, for a few moments, testing myself—then I felt the impulse to cough and did so again. I was causing it but also I wasn't. My mother said I had to get checked out, too. Our doctor's first opening was on Thursday at one p.m.

"We'll get you back in time for last period," she said.

We went to Dr. Solomon, our pediatrician, whose office was in Westwood. The nurses in his office all resembled Miss America contestants and wore the same shade of pink lipstick. Dr. Solomon always called me "Little Pumpkin" for no reason I could fathom, and I did not know how to tell him to stop. He listened to my chest and asked me to breathe.

"How is school?" he asked. "I predict the pumpkin gets all As."

I felt that hammering cough come on. It sounded like, Nnn-ka! He listened.

"Do you have something in your throat?" he asked.

I opened my mouth and he peered inside. Then he regarded me as though he just caught the tail end of a joke.

"Is the pumpkin worried about anything?" he asked.

That question itself worried me.

"Take a breath. Relax. Look around you. Enjoy!"

"What's going on?" asked my mother.

"I think this will just go away," said Dr. Solomon.

"Is she allergic to something?" my mother asked.

"The pumpkin could try meditation," he said. "Some young people I know say this works. Or maybe therapy, if it doesn't go away."

"Physical therapy?" my mother asked, frowning.

"No, talking," said Dr. Solomon. "I can give you some referrals if you want."

My face burned; how terrible this seemed. I didn't look at him or my mother as she paid the bill. I coughed in an almost elegant, desperate way.

"What's wrong?" my mother said, as she drove me to school.

"I'm fine," I said.

"But he said you were nervous about something," she said. "What?"

His words had shaken my mother; she had hoped I could just take a pill and be done, but now I could see my mother in a new light. Last year, if I had seen her hunched over the steering wheel, biting her lip, I would have thought she was shy, maybe, or determined; now I saw how anxiety filled her face, and I wished she could feel something else.

"Things," I said, feeling the coughs occupy my throat.

My mother tapped her fingers on the steering wheel.

"Do your friends bother you at all?" she asked.

I was startled by her insight; "Sometimes."

"Just avoid them if they bother you," she said. "Just walk away."

She said this in a matter-of-fact way.

"Isn't that simple?" she said. "Isn't it?"

It was not, but I felt I should agree, so that something seemed simple for her. "Okay," I said.

"Let's just see what happens," she said, and I could tell that she was trying to reassure herself. I did not want to cause her more trouble, and I tried to restrain the coughs. My jaw was very tense.

"What time is it?" I asked.

"Two," she said.

I was missing fifth period. Which was gym. Coach Huggins.

When her car pulled up at the front, I dropped out, hit the ground, zoomed toward the office. I handed the secretary my note from the doctor. She checked her watch.

"You missed fourth and fifth period," she said. "Just get the signature from your teachers and you're all set."

My parents were not superstitious people, but they were afraid I was catching my sister's allergies, or whatever they were, so they moved me out of the room. They removed everything—carpet, curtains, stuffed animals—so that the room was basically a bare cube. My new room was a large closet that was cleared out so that there was space for my twin bed. I didn't like being moved but my sister's coughing kept me up, a low, barking sound, exacerbated by the fear that I was supposed to be doing something about it (though it was unclear what). My own impulse to cough subsided when I was alone in this little room; encased in darkness, I was separate, and I was a little astonished and calmed by the smooth quiet of myself. I was afraid of the cough starting, and sometimes it did, and it kept me up, but sometimes I could just lie in bed and imagine I was assembling into something else, new, invisible. Separated from the world, I felt happy. Sometimes I thought of Tom and his long hair.

I wanted to become him. Was that what love was, was that what Laila got from sitting on Coach Huggins's lap? When I sat by Tom, the air trembled, full of glitter. In the dark, I felt the bright living rush of my desire, and I wondered if others could hear my dangerous thoughts. Then I heard footsteps through the walls and hoped they were, perhaps, Tom's, who was heroically coming to lie beside me in the little room. Or maybe they were the sounds of Ilana running around the house, for she was lost, searching for me, and I would pull her through, Ilana tired from her very long journey, I would tell her yes, she had made it, and she would thank me, glad, finally, glad to be here.

• • •

Laila had been to the beach the previous weekend and came back extremely burnt. To spend the weekend at the beach and come back bright pink was a mark of honor for the surfer group. Her face was bright pink and her eyes were slightly puffy. She gleamed, a little reptilian, with aloe vera gel.

She had gone to the beach with Coach Huggins. When she stopped by his office a few days ago, he asked her to come see him there. He was working out in Venice and she could just say hi sometime. Or, specifically, Saturday at two. If she wasn't doing anything.

There was a speeded-up quality in the way she spoke that made our group listen closely to her.

Laila's mom was going to a movie with her new boyfriend, and didn't want Laila to come because it was rated R and she shouldn't see R movies yet, so Laila took the bus to the beach. She walked down the boardwalk to the outdoor lifting area, a place we made fun of, generally, for the men were sad cartoons of men, she said, so muscled they were shaped like cubes, but there was Coach Huggins, standing in the sun, lifting up weights and lowering them.

Laila told us that Coach Huggins bought them lemonade and they walked to the beach and laid their towels beside each other. He was funny, she said. He made fun of the mothers walking by, their bathing suits, and then he pulled a towel over their legs and started touching her ankle with his finger, just like this.

She told each of us to lift our feet up on the lunch bench and then she touched the sides of our feet with her finger in a new, feathery way, and we each laughed, for we did not know how else to respond to this.

"He did *that*?" asked Jennifer, her foot jerking out in surprise.

"It was fun," Laila said. "Then."

She said this quickly, took a quick gulp of chocolate milk.

"What," we asked.

"He had a towel and he spread it over us and it was kind of cozy and we were sitting there and then we were holding hands. I liked holding hands with him. He had this nice, warm hand. And then he lifted my hand over his bathing suit and I was holding it. It was like"—she started laughing for a second, then stopped—"a big root."

The air felt as though it had become a different material, perhaps metal. We all looked at each other, pretending we understood what she meant.

Hannah clapped her hand over her mouth. "I'm sorry, what?"

"I don't want to hear this," said Audra, pressing her hands over her ears. "I don't, I don't—"

"I don't believe it," Jennifer said.

But the words were tumbling out of Laila, and she leaned forward and said, "Well, then he said oops and laughed, and then he asked if I wanted more lemonade. I said no. I said I wanted to lie out in the sun for a while, and he left and I decided I wanted to get really burned so I lay there for three hours and then went home."

She held out her arm, which was so pink it had to hurt.

"Hopefully this will turn into a tan," she said.

We stared at her. She was bragging, it seemed, but it was an aggressive sort of bragging, in which she wanted to drag us along with her; she was mad at us, for some reason, for not admiring her in the proper way.

She held out her arm again.

"Touch it," she said. "You can see your fingerprints in it."

None of us touched her arm.

"Be right back," I said.

I felt a scratchiness in my throat, I wanted something out of me, and I coughed. I didn't want them to hear, and I didn't want to be near her. I walked through the cafeteria; the other students, the flamingo plants, the silver eucalyptus standing around the cafeteria smeared by me, a blur. What happened? The junior high seemed to be inhabited by people wearing costumes, and at any moment they could fling them off and reveal other selves, like burned raw trees. I ran to my locker and opened it. The clothes for Ilana were still there, the T-shirt, the flip-flops.

There was a hand on my shoulder. I swerved around. It was Hannah.

"What are you looking at?" she asked.

I shut my locker.

"Those look too big for you."

"I'm holding them for someone."

Hannah didn't move.

"Who? Some guy?"

"No," I said.

"I have some extra clothes in my locker, too," she said. This was surprising; Hannah rarely liked to agree with me.

"For what?" I asked.

"I don't know. Something," she said.

My sister was having a difficult night and came into my little room. I felt her hand on my arm and I sat up in the dark. She took slow breaths, and I could hear the crinkling sound in her chest; it was not what I had within me. Her hair had the fragrance of lavender.

"I dreamed that you started coughing too," she said. "We sounded alike. It woke me up."

I felt that she was demeaning my own coughing situation. My discomfort was real, too.

"It was actually kind of a good dream," she said.

We were two different people, which was a confusing thing. How could the world be contoured, invisibly, in such different ways for each of us? She had the floaty, calm expression she usually wore onstage when she was landing a triple pirouette or whatever, which I admired, and which I had not seen in a while. I remembered when she was a fast runner. Before she had started coughing, we played vigorous games of tag, running in the purple twilight, turning each other into frozen statues.

"What else happened?" I asked.

She said that the air that came out of us made us rise. Then we were walking through the sky. The air felt spongy on our toes, she said, like damp bread, and we were running across it with great speed, and the glossy city sat below us.

She looked proud, because she had made that dream, and she knew what happened next in it, and I was jealous, as I wished I had dreamed it myself. I grasped her arm.

"Can I ask you something?" I said.

"What?"

"Those girls at that school. At Ma'alot. The ones they threw the grenade at."

She nodded.

"What do you think they were thinking?" I asked.

"What are you talking about?"

"Right before the grenade. When they were in the corner."

I didn't know what I wanted from her. Diane was just fourteen, two years older than I, but all of her ballet training gave her a straight, proud carriage that made her appear older than she was. She touched her tongue and picked a loose hair off it. Then she took a deep, crinkly breath.

"How to get out," she said. "I bet that's what they thought. Where can I go."

The next day at lunch, Laila was late in joining us, and Hannah, Audra, Jennifer, and I took our trays to a corner of the cafeteria far from where we usually sat. No one made a decision out loud to do this; we moved through the crowd, passing the steel table where Laila told us of her beach trip with Coach Huggins. The table now seemed sullied; none of us wanted to sit there anymore. No one mentioned Laila, though we were all thinking of her, Jennifer saying, *I think maybe she's over there?*, just once, but none of us making any effort to call her over. Instead, we watched her. She was eating a bag of popcorn for lunch. She ate it slowly, looking around. I thought of my mother saying, walk away from the friends if they bother you, and I thought, *That is what I am doing*, though I didn't think it was quite what she meant. Not one of us called her over, and not one of us said anything about this.

Laila made a slow loop near Coach Huggins. He was talking very animatedly to Avery Solon again, but not to Laila. I saw her stand in his orbit for a while, while he laughed at what Avery Solon was saying, and I watched him lift a hand to say hi to Laila, but he did not invite her to talk to him.

When I finished lunch, I waited until I saw her walk to the bathroom, and then I went to my locker. I carried my tray to the trash can and looked up and Coach Huggins was holding up a hand at me.

I froze.

He was eating an orange 50/50 Popsicle. "Hey," he said, "how's it going? Sixth period, right?"

He had never talked to me directly; I tended to stay out of his way. I nodded and tried to step around him, but he shifted slightly, so I stopped.

"Right, you're a good runner. A speeding bullet! You're that girl's friend," he said, leaning on the word "girl" so that I understood that he was pretending not to remember Laila's name. It was a familiar expression, one I had seen on the faces of the boys in my class, which meant that, for a peculiar, flickering moment, Coach Huggins looked as though he were twelve years old.

I was quiet, watchful; Coach Huggins regarded me.

"You get a chance at team captain yet?" he said.

"I don't remember," I said.

"Well, we'll check that right away. See ya later," he said, flashed that large smile, and swiftly walked away. Clutching my lunch tray, I understood, with a faint, luminous clarity and a precision that I did not yet trust, that Coach Huggins was trying to cultivate my goodwill.

In Hebrew school I was saying the V'ahavta, flying through those syllables faster than any words could be reasonably said, plunging into each long line as though it were a clear, rolling wave, lifting me through the room—my mouth was speaking almost by itself, *uchtavtam al-mezuzot bain anecha* and on and on and then I was at the end of it.

Darlene said, "Forty-seven point twenty-eight," and there was a gasp, as I had the fastest time in the classroom by a luxurious two seconds; I was the champion of the V'ahavta.

"You are the winner!" Darlene said, while the other students groaned.

Darlene pinned a blue first-place ribbon to my shirt; I fingered the thin rayon strip. Outside the smeary glass windows, a swath of bluish chaparral tumbled down the rough silver hills. I waited for the feeling of invulnerability that was supposed to come over me.

• • •

The next day our group gathered again at the new spot in the cafeteria for lunch. It felt like a regular week; Audra and Hannah ordered enchiladas in the cafeteria, Jennifer said they were gross, and we all scraped the whipped cream swirl off the tops of our cherry Jell-O. The shrieks of the other students rang through the concrete walls of the cafeteria. No one admitted that we were watching for Laila, though we were now afraid to see her. She was absent that day. And then she was absent the next. We talked—carefully—about other events at school, but no one mentioned the story she told us about Coach Huggins, the towel, and the root. We did not know how to discuss this, but after three days of Laila's absence, we did.

"She's going to miss the test in Madison's class," said Audra.

"If she misses it, she can't take it again," said Jennifer.

We were now focused on Laila's grade, and its potential to crumble into the ether.

"We should tell her," said Audra, briskly.

A few pigeons flapped around our table, pecked at the food on the ground. I think we all wished that Audra had not said that.

Each of them said they didn't have her number. I wanted to say, I didn't have her number either, but then I remembered that I did.

• • •

That night I sat in the den with my parents watching TV, waiting for the right moment to call Laila. I waited until we finished the news, and until I had finished my geometry, and after I had made my history flash cards, and then I couldn't put it off any longer and I got up and went to the phone.

I listened to the phone ring and ring and I was going to hang up, relieved that I had made an effort. Then she picked up.

"Hi," said a voice that belonged to Laila.

"Hi," I said.

"Hi," Laila said.

The moment was a pond full of lead.

"What's up?" she asked.

"I called because I just wanted to let you know that Madison's class is having a big test Tuesday. Last one before the final."

My voice had become extremely stiff and official. I felt like I was reading off a memo.

"Okay," said Laila.

"And you can't make it up."

She was quiet for a moment.

"Hello?" I said.

"I heard you," she said. "I'm just sick."

"Oh," I said, and it seemed we were agreeing on something other than this.

"I hope you feel better," I said.

I had, it seemed, transformed into a school official, which meant, then, that I was not talking to her as a friend. Laila heard this in my voice, too.

"Shut up," she said, and hung up.

• • •

The afternoon sunlight fell, gilded, on the hills; it was mid-June, the last day of Hebrew school for the year, and everyone brought snacks for a class party. It was a junk food rummage sale, with bosomy bags of Ruffles and Doritos and boxes of Entenmann's powdered donuts and Chips Ahoy! cookies piled on a desk in the corner. We were all bubbling because it was our final year of Hebrew school; the upcoming free hours on Mondays and Wednesdays seemed luxurious. Darlene smiled at us, but seemed a little remote from our exuberance; she walked around the classroom, setting postcards on a few of our desks.

"I have news. Some of the parents wrote back," she said.

It had been four weeks since we had written to the parents of the children killed at Ma'alot. I was one who received a postcard. I stared at it, and the tips of my fingers were hollow with fear.

The postcard from Ilana's parents featured a photo of the Wailing Wall in Jerusalem. The sky in the postcard was an unreal, glossy blue.

> Dear Esther, (my Hebrew name)
> Thank you very much for your note. No language has words that share our grief right now. If you come to Israel one day, come see us. You are welcome to stay in our apartment. We will show you a tree planted in her name.

I believe that you and Ilana would have been good friends.

Shalom.

My arms trembled. My own sorrow was remote from me, like an enormous tidal wave that was approaching us, slowly, a clear blue tower. It was coming to crash down on all of us; it was coming.

"I have to go to the bathroom," I said.

I left the postcard on my desk, ran to the bathroom, and sat inside a stall. I imagined I would cry or throw up, or something, but I did not. I thought of Ilana's parents, far away, missing their daughter, and for a moment it was difficult to breathe. I understood that the whole world was, in fact, an invisible cage that I could not see; I had not been aware of this cage before, but now I knew that it held me, that it held all of us, and that there was no way to get out. I was doing my weird cough—Nnn-ka! Nnn-ka!—my heart picking up, and even though these bars of the cage were invisible, they were solid, permanent. I heard myself let out a weird sound, which shook me up, and I listened to what I heard around me. There was the ringing of drops from a faucet. Each one made a clear sound, like bells.

I avoided Coach Huggins, and for this reason, I hadn't been able to get him to sign my absence slip. It was not something I could crumple up and forget about, though I wanted to—if

I didn't get his signature for this slip, he would not be able to assign me a grade.

I had to get my absence slip signed. I didn't want to do it. But I had a plan.

I stood in front of my locker and removed the clothes for Ilana, the big T-shirt, the flip-flops, the shorts. I felt both ashamed and aggressive for wearing the clothes that I had brought for her. In the locker room, I slid the big T-shirt over my head and it fell over me like a tent. I stepped into the flip-flops.

He was sitting in his little glassed office, alone, surrounded by the taped-up photos of the girl athletes, some pages curling so they were peeling off the glass.

I waited in the hallway by his office before I spoke to him. He was writing in an attendance book. He looked just like a regular person, doing this boring action. This fact alone made me pause.

He glanced up at me; I had surprised him. The hallway was long and dim and smelled of sweat, of the countless students running, jumping, trying to win.

"I have an absence slip," I called.

"Okay," he said. "Bring it over."

I wasn't sure what to do next. Bring it over. I thought this: I would walk toward him, hand him the slip with my fingers just touching the edge, watch him sign it, and then run out. I would not be here long. He squinted at me, as though he didn't quite recognize me. I probably did look strange in my long T-shirt.

I walked over, as efficiently as I could wearing flip-flops.

I heard, far away, the soft, thunderous slap of lockers being shut, the laughter echoing, flowering through the hallways, the melodic voice of Elton John. My cough came on, Nnn-ka! Nnn-ka!

"Okay," he said.

He was signing my absence slip. The ordinary nature of this action enraged me. I looked at his scalp, and I could almost count each hair.

He stood up.

He held out the slip. But not quite where I could reach it. My breath stopped. He regarded me, his face suddenly animated, and I was aware that this animation was a mask that fit neatly on his face.

He peered at me.

"What is your name?"

My name is on the slip, you idiot, I thought. I didn't want to say my name out loud. I coughed once. Nnn-ka! Another time. Nnn-ka! I sounded like a weird seal. She was moving, outside, perhaps, in the shadows. A flicker.

"She said," I whispered.

His eyebrows moved, slightly.

"What?"

"The beach," I said.

There was a slight movement in his jaw. He cleared his throat.

"You're not making sense," he said.

I coughed again. Nnn-ka!

"What's your name?" he asked, his voice sharper.

"Ilana," I said.

I was coughing now, a flutter of hammering sounds, each like a blow against the world, and he stepped back, as though I were a freak, which I was. I grabbed the slip out of his hand and walked quickly out of the room, leaving my flip-flops behind as I started to run, dropping one, then another, but I didn't stop to pick them up. "Hey!" he shouted, and it was a different hey, not the happy one. I saw him, just as I turned, looking at me, his face bewildered, but he knew, now he knew that I knew, but this was what he didn't know: who Ilana was, whose name I had borrowed for that one moment and then left on the floor of that room. I ran, even though he wasn't behind me, barefoot, down the hallway, in that T-shirt, and I imagined for that one moment that I was not myself running through the world, that I was Ilana. I was her. I imagined that I had broken out of that classroom where she had crouched, waiting with the others to die, that I, Ilana, had crawled out, opened the window, and made it outside, that I could breathe, and that now I could feel the air on my arms, oh, the air with its sweet, honey fragrance, that I was alive, I could breathe, I could hear, I could see, that I, Ilana, was still here in the world, running, alive, running.

The Pilot's
Instructions

We were sitting in the plane, waiting to back out from the gate, while the flight attendants prepared the cabin for take-off. Perplexing airplane sounds rose from unknown locations—inside the plane, out on the tarmac, in the air. It was afternoon—through the small window, the sky appeared blue and clear in a way that was both joyful and aggressive. The pilot made an announcement. "Good afternoon, everyone. Please turn off your phones or put them in airplane mode." I looked up. My fellow passengers were packed in their seats, hunched over their electronic devices as though they were all engaged in a form of prayer.

I listened to the pilot; I turned off my phone.

The cabin door slammed shut. We pretended disinterest in the person sitting next to us, though of course brimmed with many perhaps untoward thoughts about the person sitting next to us, trying not to touch each other's elbows or thighs. We all faced the same way. East. We were concerned about not reaching our destination. I didn't like flying, being strapped into a chair, gripping the plastic armrests as I looked at the world we had been separated from, briefly, far below.

I sat by the window; the passenger to my right was texting. She was long and thin, a piece of stretched gum, and appeared to be in her twenties, with short dark hair and a streak of blue on one side. The precise waviness of her hair made me think of my sister, Janine. This thought passed through me and then vanished. Her leather boots were nicer than my sneakers. She gazed at her phone with a contemplative, tender expression. Her fingers flew.

The flight attendant strode by, tossing us tiny, bright packets of pretzels. "Turn off small electronic devices and put your phones on airplane mode," she said, glancing at the passengers. How casual she was! As cheerful as carbonation, she trusted this plane, this world. There was no formal examination of the phones. It was assumed that we understood the danger. I was embarrassed that I did not. And I saw danger everywhere. In fact, I had a dream the night before that the world was about to end. It was an unoriginal movie end, with galactic disturbance and a star moving too close to Earth, but everyone here knew these were the last few days of life. It was unclear what horrible death awaited us, but it could involve fire engulfing our sweet, fragile bodies, and the sky was turning an orange gray, and we didn't know how much longer we would be able to breathe. I woke up sad and trembling. What horrible truth was the dream trying to tell me, which was sometimes a more frightening idea than the dream itself? What did the dream know that I did not? But nothing came to me. So I just got up and made breakfast, the fried eggs lacy and sizzling, bubbling in a way that reassured me.

Most of the passengers followed the flight attendant's directions with gracious obedience; I saw other phones go dark, little, dying people releasing their last breath.

The stranger beside me texted with a manic quality that was almost sexual in its focus, until she saw the smiling flight attendant walk by again, at which time she placed her phone facedown on her leg. It was a brilliant and somehow diabolical gesture. When the flight attendant had moved far enough away to miss her illicit activity, she picked it up and resumed texting. Her phone was not off. It was also not on airplane mode.

Oh my god, I thought, *she will kill us all.*

The pilot's instructions should, I assumed, be followed for a reason. I was a polite person. But I did have some people I loved whom I had scrabbled together, some family members and a few friends, and I could not bear the thought of us separated by a wall of death, not necessarily because I would miss them, which was what everyone said, and yes, I would, of course, especially when everyone was behaving well, but also because I could not bear the idea of others missing me. I wanted to be generous, but more, I wanted to have a use. Love was a form of usefulness, after all.

Plus, there were other things I wanted to do. I did want to lick frosting off cupcakes and feel air on my face and the touch of my husband's lips on my neck; I had school dance performances and recitals I wanted to attend. And I did not want to miss any orgasms expanding in me like a slow jellyfish, not one.

She continued texting.

I looked at her hands. Thumbs working hard. Fingernails painted a bright blue. Privileged hipster. I wanted to detect a history of ease in her, as though it would explain her cavalier attitude. Or maybe she had traveled her own rough path. The flight attendant was at the front of the plane, a non-enforcer of the pilot's instructions, strapping herself into a flimsy foldout seat.

And why was this passenger continuing to text? Was her message so important she would risk the lives of us all? Was it a declaration of love so absolute it surpassed any that I had felt? Was she a terrorist or perhaps just in love? What would happen if a terrorist were in love? Would he or she have second thoughts about taking down the plane? I eyed her texts. I saw a photo of a plate of spaghetti, not a particularly appetizing one, sent into the ether.

The plane began to move backward. I watched the world

slide by, the men in the orange vests standing on the asphalt, waving the vessel back. The planes resembled long, impassive animals, but they were, surprisingly, not alive. The man waving the rods, his face blank, a little sweaty, with no emotion I could discern.

Stop texting, I thought. *Stop texting. Please. Put down your phone. Put it down. Now.* I tried to tell her, firmly, with my thoughts, but she apparently didn't listen.

I did not want to be a fool. I did not want the entire plane to laugh at me. But. I did not want her to kill me with her texting, either—such an innocent-looking action, and yet.

If my life were in jeopardy, what part of my life would I speak up for?

Oh, the obvious things that people might say: the act of sitting down and eating dinner with the children, now tall as skyscrapers, and here or not, pushing out into the world, the hopeful illusion that I could nourish them when I handed over a plate with a meal on it. The feeling of my husband's hands around my hips, the silver line of desire that propelled us forward, the sorrowful, bright wound of longing in one's throat, the attempt to finally leap out of ourselves. A workplace I could depend on, not just for some months or a year but many, knowing that I had a place to go and that they appreciated what I had to contribute.

There were times when I didn't want to be alive. I'll admit that. A few times when a plane lifted off and I didn't necessarily care if it landed or not. I didn't will it to crash, but I didn't buckle my seatbelt. This felt like a statement, and a grave one.

This sorrow could be sparked by surprisingly mundane things. I don't even want to admit what they are, as they would make me look more fragile than I actually am. But even tiny things could sometimes plunge one into darkness: the intimation that you are stupid by a person whose opinion you respect. The discussion with your mother in which she revealed, after a little too much wine, that she had been more excited about your sister's birth than yours, not that yours wasn't special too (she added), and that was a little bit of a joke in the family, but also not; sometimes you wondered if your mother thought about this later, after what happened to Janine. The fact that your child, who was eighteen and living in another state, did not inform you of his new phone number after he dropped his phone in the sink. When he called you (after several days) and you yelled at him (with a dark panic that rose up like a snake), he did not talk to you for weeks. The way your body insulted you, in new and clever ways, as you got older, the times you looked in the mirror and thought you were you and other times thought you were not. Your good ideas for designing better child safety seats, which was your job, ideas that you were sure would save lives. The way you suggested these ideas, and how your superiors considered them but then quickly said no. Too expensive. Too impractical. No. And when they hired that guy who made the exact same suggestions, but in a deeper voice, they said, oh, of course. Love that. Yes.

The sensation, in short, of helplessness.

The plane kept backing out.

I remembered when I had not spoken up. Countless times,

really. The afternoon, when I was eleven, the lawns brittle but gold in the dusky light. My younger sister, Janine, darted into my room while I was getting dressed. I was just pulling my shirt over my head when she saw me, and she had never seen my breasts before. They affronted her in some way. She laughed, a sharp, terrible sound, as if I were now ridiculous, and ran out. I stood in that room, hearing that sound, and my shame made it seem my skin might peel off. She was going through a hard time then—no one on our street liked her. It was just a decision everyone made at once. I had heard one girl named Laura discussing her in soft, mocking tones and didn't correct her, because I wanted her to invite me over to her swimming pool. What was the strategy to be asked to step into that shimmering blue water?

That afternoon, Janine had been walking down the street and four of them were on their bikes. She stopped, watching them. I did too. I didn't speak. I was frozen too, I told myself. They would ride around her, I told myself, they would. Nothing else would happen to her. I felt my brain both slow down and speed up so it was, for that moment, useless, and thus I was useless, and then one of them hit her with her bike then swerved away, and she fell, with a cry that meant she was wounded in another way, and then I ran to her. Her arm was limp when I lifted her up, and she was weeping, and her arm had a dark skid on it and was broken, and the others circled around her with their bikes and watched, like vultures. I rushed her to my parents very dramatically, exclaiming with outrage about what the other kids had done, but my shame was a hard nut residing in me. I had not spoken up to stop it. For years, later, I thought my sister looked at me as though I was a clear container and she could see through it to some animal running around inside.

And I remembered the time, not long ago, a coworker called security on me. I had done nothing but wait in the office for a meeting that had never been scheduled. I just hoped that if I sat there long enough, it would begin. I had worked at the company for six years and the supervisor of my department, a man with a head the precise shape of an egg, had said a week before, looking down, shyly, as if he were asking me on a date, that they would not be able to pay me for my work anymore. They were tightening their budget. I had done nothing wrong. I thought of showing him my checking account, wondering if that would make him change his mind, but I did not. I thought about what he said and the next day, I walked into the office because there was no one watching and I sat in the conference room waiting for the meeting that I was not supposed to attend because I did not work there anymore. I sat with my files and presentation, waiting five minutes then ten, then fifteen, walking around the room and touching the black vinyl chairs, wondering who would be sitting in them, what they would think of me, then noticing the secretary watching me through the glass, walking in and asking, her voice trembling, "Are you waiting for someone here today?" She had put in my termination paperwork the day before. I should have said, "Arnold," the head of the department, "I would like to meet with Arnold to discuss plans for the week." Just saying that in a determined voice would have made them think yes, what idiots we are, we must promote her and fire these other three employees instead! But I did not speak up. I sat in a chair, waiting. A couple of flies began to buzz around me, as though I were dead. I swatted them away, but they kept coming, with a curious intent. The security guard, a man named Henry, came into the room, examining me with a puzzled expression, for he had seen me walk into this office many times before, but now I was not supposed to be here. And the security guard stared at me in shock with, I thought, the same expression as my sister; perhaps he, like Janine, running into my room many years ago, had seen something peculiar and troubling in me.

I still felt the guard's hand, firm, on my shoulders as I walked out. He had a large hand, and his grip was oddly paternal, but it was just firm enough to tell me I was not allowed there anymore.

That was another time I had not spoken up for myself.

I thought of, years ago, the time I drove around, looking for the person I thought I loved. I was too embarrassed to ask him the location of the restaurant where we were supposed to meet. We knew each other as classmates, at our university, where we both took courses in beginning French, and practiced ordinary conversations in which he was a shopkeeper and I tried to buy an orange, a baguette, and a chicken, and then I was a doctor and he tried to ask for a shot. This was a few months after my sister had been killed (a bike ride, rushing off from her job, wearing no helmet, the part I did not understand), and I was in a daze in which I did not want to converse in English, which was my language of daily life. It just felt wrong to say anything in this language at all; it described nothing precise about the world. I took French because I liked the way it sounded. I met a student there who wanted to practice with me after class. There was something in our fake conversations that made me feel ridiculously alive, as though we actually briefly became the shopkeeper or coffee shop owner or doctor or teacher in the study guide, even though we could barely sound out the syllables, though sometimes we would, and it made me think that our conversations in English would free me in the same way, that we would become larger and more beautiful versions of ourselves. The way his bronze hair gathered in the sun made me want to touch it.

And then one day, after our semester had ended, he asked me to go to dinner, in French, and then he said to meet at this restaurant, at this time; he laughed in the way that made me think we understood each other, and I thought I understood all of it, but I was so full of anticipation and the hope that I would feel differently talking to him, I said yes, I would meet him there. But he was not at that restaurant, and when I called him he said,

"I am here." In French.

But he was not there. I didn't want to use English. I said I would be there soon. But where? I got in my car and drove around, but I couldn't find the restaurant. And I was so set on not asking him in English, not revealing how much I did or did not actually understand in French, I called back and asked him, "Where are you?" in French.

He sounded a little weary and gave me the address.

So I drove around that night, making stops at the restaurants on the street he mentioned, and then other neighboring regions, but he was nowhere to be found. I just drove around the city, through the darkness, and felt the permanence of his absence, and of my sister's, and that night, I felt a little bit of myself vanish. I never saw him again.

I didn't speak up the right way, or in a way that was at all effective, when my mother asked me to find out what had happened to my sister. The accident happened when Janine was riding her bike from the optometrist's office where she worked. We had many questions about the accident. Why was she riding away so fast? Where was she going? Why was she not wearing a helmet? Did something happen at the optometrist's office so she was rushing away in fear? Or was she just, more boringly, not looking where she was going? My mother sat at the kitchen table and repeated these questions, every day, her longing a shovel, digging into air. She wanted to scold my sister, but there was no one there to scold. Here I was, with my mother, in the sour light of the den; Janine was not in the other room, and never would be, and we sat, waiting and not waiting, in that peculiar frozenness of the living after a death. I listened to my mother ask, in a circular way, what had happened, for we did not know how to think, neither of us. I wanted to do something. One day she said,

"You."

"What?"

"You should go ask," she said. "Go to the office. Find out."

She wanted this from me, so I did it. I am a shy person, so this assignment was not easy for me. I went to the office and pretended I was making an appointment for a new prescription. But my eyes were 20/20, and had always been. My sister was the person in the office to help you choose frames. She was excellent at figuring out how frames would transform your face.

I remembered when we were maybe in our twenties, looking for Janine's first pair; she was strangely excited by the idea of getting glasses. She thought they were a form of self-revelation. Janine's face was small and delicate, and most pairs we found were too big for her face. Finally I found a pair that seemed completely unlike her—a pair of circular plastic frames, in burgundy—but when she looked at herself in the mirror, her face lit up. "Yes," she said. "Yes! I love it." She looked at me, setting the frames evenly, and she did seem somehow transformed, older. She looked happy to be who she was.

"Now you," she said, and though I didn't wear glasses, she picked out a pair of frames that were blue and fancy in a way I would never choose—"This." I put them on, and the glasses revealed in me a sweeping authority; others would certainly now listen to me.

"What do you think?" she asked.

"Yes," I said. I appreciated the fact that she could see this in me. She bought her glasses and we walked out.

Where was that moment now? I missed her, terribly; how I wanted to stand with her on that moment, a floe of ice.

It seemed impossible that the office was open and operating as usual, though that was their right. Janine had worked in this office less than a year. When I walked in, the receptionist greeted me as though I were simply a patient; she saw nothing similar between my sister and myself, even though we shared the same eyes. With that greeting, I felt not just the finality of Janine's absence, but the ephemeral nature of the receptionist herself, the potted palm in the corner, all of us. It was a cold slap. The receptionist showed me into the examination room.

Who did it, I thought, as I met the optometrist's assistant, who put drops in my eyes, and the optometrist, who peered at my eyes through the metal contraption. I was a few inches from their faces. Their eyes resembled eyes. They simply went about their business, asking me which letter I could see more clearly. This or this.

This or this.

Neither.

What was the explanation, I thought. *What happened to Janine? Why did she bike off that way?* I pushed away the optometrist's machine and sat forward.

"I don't need these," I said.

They looked at me, wary and surprised.

I said my sister's name. I said, "What happened? We want to know what happened. Why did she ride off so fast? Do you know? We want to know."

This was, of course, the first problem. I was not strategic or smooth or intelligent; I did not have the time for it, I just blurted this out, in this ineffective way. The optometrist and assistant glanced at each other; I could not penetrate their expression, whether it revealed fear about my sister or about me. They said Janine's name.

"Oh, that was terrible," said the optometrist. "She took her bike and my god."

"We were just talking about her shoes and where she bought them," the assistant said. "And then. Oh. I'm sorry. That was such a shock."

They stood, perplexed and human, mouthing sympathy, but they didn't have an answer for me. I peered at them, looking for evidence of knowledge or wrongdoing, but I saw nothing in their faces that would tell me more.

"I wish I had known her better," the assistant said, wistfulness in her voice.

This was her answer. More questions pressed into my throat and I wanted to ask the one that would shake them, that would give me some bit of information on anything, for my mother, about what had happened. I wanted to ask them why I had not been able to help her that afternoon when we were children, why I had been so poisoned by my own shame. I wanted to ask it all. But I didn't, as they seemed sad, too, standing there, rumpled, hands empty.

I drove home, and wanted to pick up something on the way; I rushed into the supermarket and bought some apricots; I was halfway home when I remembered that this was Janine's favorite fruit. When I walked into the house, I saw my mother on the couch, gazing at me with a dreadful hope. I handed her an apricot, and she held it in her hand for a moment, feeling its softness. Their sweet orange fragrance floated into the air.

I didn't like the silence between us, so I said, "They said she was in love."

My mother's face shifted slightly, a little bit awake. "With who?"

"They didn't know."

We sat together in this flimsy, manufactured shelter—of what? This wouldn't solve anything; there was nothing to learn. My mother slowly ate her apricot; she seemed a little bit comforted. Each day melted into the next.

But I was aware of my failure in finding out why my sister had ridden off that way. I felt that curdle within me.

That was years ago; I wasn't sure why I was thinking about this now. But here we sat, the stranger who had hair like my sister's, and I waited for her to follow the pilot's instructions so that we could all continue to live. The plane was poised at the runway, about to take off. She still texted, sending off messages.

The flight attendants were chatting; one had flown all night from Madrid.

The inside of my palms were a little wet.

I imagined myself making a joke about her phone; perhaps that would make her stop. "Hey, don't want to send us off to Antarctica, do you?" I could say, referring to the plane's navigation system. I was not, despite my obsessions, a weirdo; I could be funny. She would laugh and nod and instantly turn the thing off.

I watched her fingers move across the phone. I wondered whom she loved and who loved her, and whom she wished she could talk to, and whom she could not.

Which tweet, which word would lead to the plane malfunction? To our end?

She glanced up at the window and then back.

"Please close the window," she said, flatly.

I was surprised by her voice. Clipped, like a substitute teacher's. She had no problem asking me for anything.

I took a breath, but the words wouldn't come.

The aircraft parked at their gates, the dark windows along the sides, the people peering out at the dingy air, the large men on the asphalt waving them to their futures. What were they eating, I wondered.

"What?" I asked.

"Can you?" she asked. "I don't like to see the plane take off."

I quietly processed this request. This was what she feared. How could she be afraid of that while willfully ignoring the pilot's instructions? Everyone's fear was its own intricate and rule-bound world. None of it made sense.

I tried to think about how to respond to this.

"No," I said.

She stared at me.

"And why not?"

"I want to see us take off," I said.

"Seriously?" she asked. She twisted around, with some difficulty, in her tiny seat.

The stranger beside me had no idea that she looked familiar, or dangerous. I couldn't stand it anymore—I wanted to grab the phone and tell her: don't bring down the plane. Let it float to its destination. Let me out.

"Stop texting," I said, quickly. "The pilot said to stop."

There.

She looked at me coolly, the way a person does when she can suddenly see all the way through you, to the booming raw heart of yourself. I tensed.

Then she laughed.

"They always say that," she said. "Don't believe them."

"Why not?"

"It's silly."

"We're about to put this thing in the air," I said, curtly. "It's not natural. I always believe them."

"It's how the airlines maintain power," she said. "It's totally fake. But they make us afraid and dependent and then we pay exorbitant fees for our luggage."

She appeared cheerful and resolute in these theories. But why? How were these issues connected? Was this in *Consumer Reports*? She had clearly thought about this; she delivered all of this with an earnest face.

"I don't believe it," I said. "And I want the plane to stay in the air."

She regarded me with a long, gooey gaze of pity; then she sighed and pressed her thumb against her phone. It shut off.

She had done what I had asked. The phone was off and the plane was perhaps safe. Relief rushed through me like sweet air. Perhaps I would get to my destination. I would have another day.

The plane began to rush forward, with a purpose. We held still in the solemn way that passengers did when the plane was about to lift off the earth. My teeth trembled.

Then I thought—why had I been so afraid of this texting? Why did our fear land any particular place? And, finally, more to the point, what was wrong with me?

"Thank you," I said. I loved her, immensely, for a moment. This feeling leapt out of me briefly, a leopard that had been caged.

"Now," she said. "Can you close the window?"

"Yes," I said. "I will."

I glanced out the window. The plane was coasting. What else could I ask for? How much could I ask for?

I held the little foil bag of pretzels the flight attendant had tossed to us. I wanted a pretzel at that moment, so I tore open the bag and chewed one, noisily. The texter looked at me, with a mournful expression, and I realized she was hungry. Her pretzel bag was nowhere to be seen. I silently held out my foil bag and shook a pretzel into her palm and we sat beside each other, crunching the pretzels. It was a pleasant sound. We sounded exactly alike.

Bright light came through the curved square windows and shadows trembled on the inside of the plane. The sun fell upon all of us, trapped in our seats, the light lovely on our hair. I could feel the speed in my jaws. The stranger beside me closed her eyes. I put my hand on the window shade, but before I shut it, I looked outside. There was the world, below me. It was endless and silent as we rose. The mountains looked like islands in the ruffled, white-cloud sea.

The Department
of Happiness and
Reimbursement

The first time I went to 140 Standard Street, the location of
my new office, I walked slowly, observing the many people
in business suits moving through the skyscrapers' long cool
shadows, and I wondered, passing by them, which workers
were real. There were messengers on bikes, weaving around
the pedestrians. There were people carrying large cardboard
boxes out of trucks and into stores. The general sense of noise
and activity made it seem that our country was productive and
busy. I was surprised at the activity, because I had been told

that many of the downtown buildings were empty, that lights were set on a timer to wink on and off to simulate people inside these offices. There were rumors that some were hired to pretend to walk into and out of buildings, to make it appear that labor was ongoing. I tried to guess who had a job, and who was only wearing a costume. I wondered if the newness of their suits would tip me off, or the way they clutched their cups of coffee, or the vacant quality of their stares. We all regarded one another, warily, wondering who here had a purpose and who was imitating those who did. But the distinctions didn't matter; all of us were, I knew, glad to be allowed downtown. It was better, we thought, than the alternative, and we walked across the sidewalk, swiftly, faces set in expressions that did not reveal our fear.

The Department of Employment Services was enclosed in a large, boxy, concrete building that, in its impenetrability, resembled a face with eyes shut. It was a few miles from the Capitol. No one in the office wanted anyone to know where we were located, so the building was not marked and the windows, from the street, appeared dark. Inside, the structure was old and in need of repair. The fluorescent rods on the ceilings sometimes flashed and went out forever, the plaster in the wall by the water fountain was discolored as though someone had once punched a hole in it, doors fell off hinges, the carpets emanated an odor of stale donuts and death, and there was a general dimness in the building; we operated, at all hours, in dusk.

The number of jobs in our great nation had dropped

drastically in recent years. The administration's solution to this was to keep people in their current jobs, sometimes with force. The administration wanted those without jobs to yearn for them, and, also, did not want the unemployed to know what many of the current jobs actually entailed. As employees often had complaints, on a wide range of topics, the government's response was a onetime financial reimbursement, with the caveat that the complaints would remain secret and never be shared. I had no idea why I was one of the few selected for this department—my essay skills weren't that great, and universities were still churning out students, thousands each year, for the foundation of a productive nation was the ability to manufacture hope. I had made a point of this in my essay, the redemptive powers of hope in our great country, of the ways we could be generous to one another. This last point, I would later learn, is what prompted Mr. Watson to hire me.

I could tell almost no one that I found a job. I said that I was going to visit a relative in Maryland who needed help. That was an acceptable answer—it was what many recent graduates ended up doing—moving in with frail, ancient relatives who were trying to live on nothing and had an extra room. There was a special interest in relatives who were very ill and barely ate, thereby allowing the graduated students to eat their rations. Telling others about my job could be dangerous; some friends who had graduated with me and found work had been followed to their place of employment and attacked. This was a trend I was hearing about—those who followed the fortunate ones, and, when they were alone, broke their legs with a steel rod. It was a swift, efficient operation. While the injured workers recovered, the attackers would slip in a résumé. This strategy sometimes worked.

When I was hired, my supervisor liked to refer to us as the Department of Happiness and Reimbursement, but really I was an assistant in the Office of Workplace Grievances. My task was to read the complaints and organize them by profession, state, city, and amount of reimbursement. There were many to process, every day.

> I've been a kindergarten teacher for seventeen years and we pass three books around the classroom, sixty kids. When I started, there were just eighteen kids in class. I had an assistant until a child bit her and her bite got infected and there was no medicine available and she died.

> These are my hours: Monday at noon to Wednesday at noon, without stopping. Then Thursday to Saturday, same. I'm so tired my boss knows I hate it. He says my schedule is easier than most. He schedules me for it every week. I never see my child. I don't get to take her to school. I'm stuck. The other restaurant is fifteen miles away and I don't have a car. I am so tired I could fucking die.

I have to stand naked by the interstate. I
thought it was because I have a nice body
though I'm advertising an auto repair shop.
I want to put my foot down at standing like
this in weather under 60 degrees. It gets cold.
At least I should be able to wear a sweater.
People throw food at me or yell things.

I would sort the complaints (wages, long hours, exploitive
overtime, terrible bosses and colleagues, unhealthy working
conditions, etc.), send them to the reimbursement office, receive the amount, and then call up the workers who sent in the
complaint and inform them of their claim amount. Mr. Watson
had perceived generosity in me, in my voice and my essay (generosity was highly valued in this work and mentioned often in
department memos and signs), and had coached me in talking
with workers about their reimbursement. I had a natural voice
for this, he said. I sounded like someone they could trust.

"Your reimbursement is $1,208," I said.

Or—"Your reimbursement is $872."

Or "You will receive a check for $2,509."

"The investigation is ongoing."

I would hear the pause and shout of joy or Yes! Or Yeah,
baby! Or Thank you, God! Or Bless you, honey!

As instructed, I held the phone and counted to three. I was
supposed to pretend to listen, to show that we, the government
of our great nation, cared, though the truth was that I actually
did listen. I sat in my office, cabinets so crammed with files

they wouldn't close, eavesdropping on this brief moment of joy. It felt real, this joy, and I wanted to hear what that was like. I was proud that I had helped enable this joy, that I was earning a salary, and that this was my vital contribution.

When I went into the office for my initial interview, I sat in front of Mr. Charles Watson, who had been working in the federal government for many years. He told me, slowly and gravely, that there was nothing to be done about the workers' situations. Some in Congress thought that there were solutions, but they were people who were unreasonable and soft. The job market was shrinking; this was just a fact. A lucky few would, through the national game show, be rewarded; be happy for them. It was unfortunate that some workers ended up in situations that they didn't like for their own sad reasons. "Nations," he said, "reinvent themselves. Some people evolve with it. For them, rejoice!" Mr. Watson was a solid man with thin gray hair, who had a transparent quality about him even though he was sitting, quite solidly, at his desk. But when he spoke of the workforce, his attitude changed, and suddenly he seemed to be wearing a sparkling, diamond suit, though his actual suit was always gray. The difficulties and struggles of others provided a mirror for him to reflect upon his own achievements, as they were; he almost glittered when he spoke of the sorry workforce. I didn't know much about him. He talked about his mother in a nursing home outside the Capitol; sometimes he picked up dark red roses for her, even though she didn't know him now, but she reached out to touch the roses each time he brought them.

Mr. Watson called me in sometimes to discuss the state of the nation. I listened, or I tried to look like I was listening, something I knew how to do. What I heard, mostly, in the rapid, hushed anger of his words, was an anticipation so weighted, the air felt dense, like a pound cake. He appeared to be waiting for something significant. I believed he had been waiting for this for years.

But then. We were talking about those who did have jobs, but were not happy in them. He told me that there had been studies done on what was called "the disgruntled worker," there were studies done on workplace shootings, of the cumulative effect of silence on workers, and what he called the "productivity cost" of holding everything in.

"You think people get sick because of loneliness, or their family, et cetera, and they do, sometimes." But mostly, he said, "They are mad at work. They would be worse off *not* at work, as we know, but there at least they hold on to the hope of somehow getting a job. When they are at the office, they see what they're paid, what they are required to do, what other people get. They feel things are unfair. This is a sad and general perception." He paused. "So we are here to help."

Mr. Watson had many thoughts on generosity, which he shared with me. "One thing I have learned from my years in government," he said, "is the way my nation has showed me the goodness in myself. An unveiling, as it were. I didn't realize it when I began, long ago, but I realized it when I saw the

vast resources of our department. Look at what we could do!
We could solve problems. Others needed to be grateful to us."

I, too, wanted to be viewed as a good person. I was sending money back to my family, my dues for my luck in finding
this position. I was the oldest of five, and my brothers and sister were still in school; if my family appeared to have enough
money, if they seemed to be useful, no one would be sent to
the Compounds. My parents worked for a time but had no
jobs at the moment (my mother going on two years, my father
four), and my contribution helped make them appear to be
still employed. *I bought a new suit,* my mother wrote to me,
*A navy blazer with rhinestone buttons and pants. In case any-
one calls, I'm ready! I got a haircut last week. A nice cut, short,
professional. It's good for people to see.* I clutched the phone and
listened to my voice roll through, and I wondered, flickeringly,
what happened to those who sent in complaints after I hung
up, if this reimbursement helped them; I also wondered sometimes what was happening to me.

I usually left the office at 6:30, walking along the streets outside the Capitol, past the real workers and those who were paid
to pretend. I boarded a train back to my apartment, and my
route took it, at one point, by one of the Compounds; it picked
up speed and passed the wall with such force, the whole train
car rattled. The Compounds were set up behind enormous
concrete walls, so no one outside could see inside them. The
people who lived there were unemployed, probably forever.

They received a limited amount of money each month and food rations, which varied with each new administration. No one knew exactly what they did all day, but there were reports that some Compounds had conditions worse than others, that there was illness left untreated to diminish the numbers of people to feed, that the government did not maintain decent plumbing or water, that houses were crumbling and full of rot. Occasionally, explosions rumbled through some of the Compounds, but no one explained why this was. The point was that there were too many people and not enough for them to do, so all the leftover people were moved into the Compounds.

What the people in the Compounds could participate in was the national game show. *Your New Home* united the country once a week, regardless of employment; I didn't know anyone who didn't watch. The national game show was a trivia quiz designed by committees of a cross-section of America— construction workers and housekeepers and college professors and scientists and artists and lawyers—it was democratic in this way. But once a week, someone from each city's Compound won this quiz, and went on to regional quizzes, competing with others who won within their Compounds, and these people appeared on the show, and once a week someone in the nation would win.

The prize was a mansion, usually one that had been abandoned. They were located in cities all over the country: on the beach in Malibu, for example, on a snowy mountain overlooking Boulder, in a New York skyscraper, in a suburb of Atlanta. The mansions were the focus of everyone's yearning. Huge monuments of real estate, with ten bedrooms or more, swimming pools shaped like lagoons, tennis courts, vast green gardens. Some resembled Tudor mansions, some were Spanish villas, some French chateaus, some shaped like cubes. There were groups dedicated to refurbishing the mansions, and decorating them, and part of the game show was a detailed tour of the mansion to be won that day. One episode was dedicated simply to a mansion's closets, showing the various ways a person could store dresses or shoes. A winner was decided each week. Fifty-two winners a year. And then, in an episode that was thrilling every time, the winner and their family were airlifted out of the Compounds to their new home and a generous stipend for life.

The entire family would be blindfolded, and the most moving part of *Your New Home* was when the blindfolds were taken off and they walked through the gleaming hallways of the home where they would spend their lives. Every family cried with joy, in a show of emotion that felt cathartic for the nation. We were envious but also relieved that this could happen to someone. Each family became celebrities for a few months, as they adjusted to their new life of comfort, and there were episodes dedicated to how they would furnish their new house, funny arguments about different types of couches or dishes or bedspreads. There was one segment in which a family had a screaming argument about whether to buy Waterford or Mikasa or Spode plates, though in fact they had the fortune now to buy a set of each of them. It culminated with a furious mother-in-law hurling a Waterford pitcher out the window and a dramatic slow-motion arc as the pitcher crashed on the sidewalk below. That slow-mo arc of the doomed pitcher was all anyone talked about for a week. Everyone in the nation yearned to have such arguments. The producers of the show enjoyed airing video of the audience. Across the nation, the camera panned over all of us—the unemployed in the Compounds, faces brilliant with hope as they tried to answer correctly, and the employed, watching them play the game. All of us together watched a winner step out of the limo and, hand trembling, open a mansion's shining door.

Shortly after I started at the Department of Happiness and Reimbursement, there was a review of the employees on our floor, and four out of ten were, as they said, "released." This happened on a Friday, and by Monday they were gone. A chill fluttered through the department. There was much whispering about why the four were fired—some said they submitted reimbursements that were too extravagant; some said they were not saying "Good luck!" firmly enough to turn people away. Sometimes frustrated workers called back, demanding more money, claiming that they did not know the reimbursement was a onetime event. A man once cleverly discovered the location of our office and stood outside of it, shouting, "What the hell, you stingy assholes, nothing's changed. Nothing! Give me more." We cowered inside the building, watching him from a window, unsure what he was planning to do, and impressed by the raw rage in his voice; no one could express that sort of feeling in the office. The man was quickly arrested.

The department, Mr. Watson reminded us, was a place of generosity. But also of clarity and closure.

One afternoon, Mr. Watson came into my office and told me that I was being moved downstairs. "It's actually a promotion," he said. "You need more space." I did need more space; the file cabinets were stuffed with files and would not shut, even if I pushed on them, leaning on a drawer with my shoulder. He led me to an office in the basement, which, in addition to the sputtering fluorescent lights, held the dark, wet odor of earth. It did not seem like a promotion; I wondered what was going on.

"We need, well, a woman in this office," said Mr. Watson.

I was a woman, yes, but I almost laughed. He appeared concerned.

"There has been an uptick in complaints of a particular nature," he said. "We need someone who will be . . ." He paused. "Sensitive to issues at hand."

He brushed some dust off a crack in the wall. I would not describe myself as "sensitive," though I pretended I was, every day, every call I made, and felt fraudulent that this random and unearned status of womanhood qualified me for this promotion. It seemed the easiest qualification I had ever had, and the most puzzling.

The next day, when I came to work, movers had efficiently relocated all of my office furniture and items on my desk—the photos of my family, the cactus in the pot—and set them up, exactly as they had been, in my new office. They were clearly ready for me to get to work. There was a sense of dark gloom in the basement, as there was almost no one down here. Some of the empty offices were used for storage, stuffed with old steel desks and swivel chairs. One slow, creaky elevator lifted us to the first floor.

That week, I noticed other women were also moved down to the basement—they were my age, early twenties. We did not approach each other at first—we seemed to have been selected for a certain shyness, or aloofness, and also an overly muscular diligence, as we spent a great deal of time shut in our offices, organizing filing systems, before the complaints came in. It took us a week to introduce ourselves to each other. There was Kayla, Marianne, Jana, and I; we were from different parts of the nation, and this was the first job for all of us.

When we spoke, we marveled at the similarity of our voices. Though we had slightly different accents—mine was California, Kayla was Houston, Marianne was New York, Jana was Iowa—our voices shared the same honeyed quality. We sounded freakishly kind, even if perhaps we were not. We laughed as we listened to each other, but I believed we were a little unnerved by this, too.

Even though I was glad to be promoted, and to be part of this new division helping our great country, I began to dread the moment I heard the elevator open, as the mail person brought the new load of complaints for the day. For there were many. There were complaints from every corner of the nation, from every industry.

> Help me make it stop. I work in the kitchen and when I bend over to pick up a bag of frozen fries my boss grabs my ass and says I want a bite of these juicy buns and I have to wait till he's not around to get the fries and then people are yelling for their fries because no one can fucking wait for their fries ever and I get in trouble please help me.

> I clean rooms at the Economy Suites and I can't go on floor six because he's waiting for me pretending to check the ice machine but waiting until I get into a room and then once he came in and I fought him off I can't go to work floor six hasn't been vacuumed in two weeks because I can't go to floor six.

Each morning, I opened the envelopes that held these new kinds of complaints. There were many more than before, and all the complaints came from women, and though I struggled to maintain my efficient pace, I found myself slowing down. I could only read a few at a time before I found myself getting tired. It was a tiredness that seemed to reside in the very center of my bones, that seemed to imply I had run many miles, although I was simply sitting at my desk, reading and sending complaints on for reimbursement.

I went through the files and met my coworkers each afternoon by the elevator. Our files were confidential, and we were not supposed to discuss them with each other, but we did, in urgent whispers, while we waited for the elevator, before we stepped back into the world.

"What did you have today?"

"Numerous ass grabs in Ohio. Food industry."

"If you're ever in an office in Houston, stay away from closets."

The hours of listening and saying, in our kind, extremely sensitive tones, "We will begin an investigation and we will inform you shortly of your reimbursement," in response to women shouting at us or sobbing or whispering so we could barely hear them, was more grueling than any of us would admit.

Kayla stepped close to us. "One woman in Michigan, her boss liked to taste his female workers. Lick them on the neck."

We buttoned our coats tightly as we considered this.

"Mine pretended to whisper something to his worker and then slipped a hand into her shirt, just for a second. Sometimes just before meetings. He believed they'd be distracted when he did that. But not in the way he thought."

"That's nothing," whispered Marianne, who seemed to derive a kind of status when she described her cases. "I had two different women in one office file claims about the same guy. He pretended to go into the wrong bathroom, grab the worker who was in there, kiss her, and rush out. I'm not kidding."

"Where was this?" asked Kayla, as though searching for regional logic.

"Nebraska," said Marianne.

"Nebraska," said Kayla, nodding. Our talk about complaints were a sort of armor—if we talked about them, if we learned something, perhaps these incidents would not happen to us. For as we gathered by the elevator, sharing what we knew, housed in the shelter of our own alleged generosity, we did not confess what kept us staring into the dark at night— that we did not know how to stop any of this. And we had no idea how reimbursing these women would help.

The elevator wheezed, tiredly, away from the basement.

"How much do you think they'll get?" I asked.

"Depends on the complaint," Marianne said. "Gross comments, I don't know, a hundred dollars. If the comments were made just once or constantly—more then. Actual physical contact, a thousand dollars. Worse things, I don't know. What is the department's budget?"

"Not big enough," Jana said.

"Do you have trouble reading them?" I asked.

The complaints floated into my dreams. I woke up some nights and heard myself calling out; it seemed that a cool, disembodied hand was reaching inside every bit of me. I woke up, embarrassed by the yelp I made. The women making the complaints were entering my body in their own way and engaging in a variety of behaviors, which included screaming at the people who harmed them and sometimes stabbing them with large knives. When I woke up, it never felt as though I had slept.

"I think about how much we can give them," said Kayla, sounding hopeful. "I imagine their happiness when they hear me say how much they will get."

"Why can't they just move them to other jobs?" asked Jana. "Get them out of there."

"Jana, quiet," whispered Kayla. "Where would they go?"

The elevator stopped, with a shudder, and the force jolted through my bones.

"But," said Jana.

The doors of the elevator opened. We walked out into the street's glaring light and arranged our faces into the delicate expressions of workers who wanted to be identified as workers, but not definitively so; we did not want to attract jealousy or violence.

After hours in the low, false light of the basement, it took a few minutes to adjust to the sun, the clamorous bustle of the street. Each time I walked out of the building, it was difficult to look closely at anyone. There was a silent code governing the actions of others, and I wanted to understand it, through the smallest gestures—the way the man stood behind me at the stoplight, waiting for me to step first, the way the woman at the deli counter handed me a coffee, the way we walked around each other on the sidewalk. There was nothing to learn. The air was silent, but full as a balloon. People scrubbed the sides of the buildings so they shone. Pale soap bubbles glittered in the gutters. My coworkers and I walked together for a block or two before going to our different train stations, and I could tell the others were looking at people's faces the way I was—wondering not just which workers were real, not just that, but imagining what light or darkness everyone held inside of them, and what our deep and capacious generosity could do.

The first reimbursements were ready, and we gathered in Kayla's office around a large stack of yellow envelopes. We were very interested in what the Office of Happiness and Reimbursement thought the remuneration for these complaints should be.

We each opened one. My fingers trembled.

$53.

$40.

$125.

$15.

Jana gasped.

I checked these reimbursements against the complaints. They seemed surprisingly meager compared to the amounts I had distributed previously. We looked at the amounts and though none of us wanted to be designated as too generous (we did not want to be viewed as extravagant), we could not hide our reactions; we were shocked.

"Maybe these are typos," Kayla said.

"I think we should check," said Jana. "For accuracy."

"You really think this is wrong?" asked Marianne. "Ha. I think this is what they are going to get."

Marianne folded her arms in front of her, a gesture of authority. She liked to appear the most realistic of the group, which meant the harshest; it gave her a certain standing among us. But her comment made us anxious.

"If this is what we are telling them," said Kayla, "at least they should pay us more."

We decided that one of us should go talk to Mr. Watson, and they decided that person should be me. Kayla told me how to ask. Not with anger. Reasonably. We wanted, of course, to be accurate. Perhaps the reimbursements were missing one zero or even two.

I took the elevator to the sixth floor, Mr. Watson's office.

"I received these," I said, holding out the first reimbursements, "and our department wondered if they were correct."

Mr. Watson took the files from me and looked them over. He nodded and handed them back.

"What do you think they should be?"

"I don't know. They appeared to us as a bit low—"

Mr. Watson smiled, a smile that implied great patience.

"Miss Windham, you do know how many complaints of this type we are getting in each week," he said.

"Yes. I read them," I said.

"And you know that our budget is limited," he said. "Certainly we would like to help them, of course, we know they have had a terrible experience, or so they claim. Let me tell you in confidence that the number of these complaints, or the *del-*

uge of them, has led to, well, some questioning in upper levels of our department of their authenticity. We are drowning in these complaints, Miss Windham. We have to be realistic. We have, in fact, a budget. I can't just snap my fingers and create money. We simply cannot spend much, even if, and I say if, every single one of these claims is true."

He did not look at me as he said this. I turned just slightly to see where his gaze was going—it fell on a window, the light a glowing square within it, nothing.

"I am concerned that these reimbursements are not enough," I said.

"Well, they will have to be," he said. "We all have things we wish were different. When my mother looks at me, Miss Windham, she sees my brother. It has been a year since she has remembered my name. I do not know why."

He glanced at his hands, which were clasped tightly together; they appeared glossy, made of glass.

"This is just to say that we all have our unhappiness and seventy-two dollars is a lot for some people. A nice dinner. A pair of shoes. A little something that will make them feel better. Do you know the power of these rewards, Miss Windham? The brain reacts in a positive way. It can erase negative thoughts and experiences. You know that people cling to their discomfort," he said. "I believe it's a form of amusement. Life is hard. People have to just embrace the *good*." He stood up, suddenly, went to the file cabinet, opened one up, and brought out a handful of letters. "Here," he said. "People are glad to get something. For example, I can tell that you are glad for this job, Miss Windham." He leaned toward me across his desk. "I can see it in the efficient way you work through your files. That gives me hope."

"Thank you," I said. My heart was the size of a grapefruit. "I have hope, too. We were thinking, perhaps, that the size of the reimbursements might be met with resistance from those filing their complaints. We hoped that perhaps our own salaries might be raised, for this may be challenging to deal with."

Mr. Watson unclasped his hands.

"I will look into our budget for possible bonuses," he said. "Thank you for alerting me. The reimbursements, though, will have to stand."

My coworkers were encouraged to hear about our possible bonuses, though they still could not believe the reimbursements were correct. Jana wondered if I had asked Mr. Watson the right question, which I found insulting. Kayla wondered if he had misheard, and Marianne was the only one who believed his answer was true. We each had a stack of packets. No one wanted to start calling the women about their reimbursements. We each claimed we would start calling that day, but across the office I saw various forms of procrastination—Kayla moving a hand vacuum over her carpet, Jana alphabetizing her files and asking if she could organize mine as well, Marianne making a thorough survey of her office supplies. We were a frenzy of activity around nothing.

We spent one Friday afternoon, when no one stopped by the basement, watching *Your New Home*. A man from Texas won that day. The host of the show, Harry Cash, was taking Mr. Plummer and his family to see a mansion in California, in Malibu, the sort of house that resembled a giant ice cube, with dark gray glass, set right on the beach.

From Marianne's office we watched Mr. Plummer and his wife, four children, his mother, an aunt, and two cousins stroll through the rooms, faces turned in an almost painful wonder, at the display of luxury—the bathrooms with porcelain Jacuzzi tubs overlooking the ocean, the bedrooms with beds the size of boats, the balconies where the ocean wind dramatically lifted their hair. They had made it. They would never worry again about work or money. They began to cry, all of them, and the elderly mother dropped to her knees and kissed the marble floor and cried, "Thank you, Lord!" and the children began to run onto the beach, running and running, the sun glinting on the ocean in a way so painfully beautiful it made my forehead hurt with longing. Harry Cash put his arm about Mr. Plummer, who looked at his new home and said, "Thank you. Thank you."

His gratitude rose off him like a terrible heat. We all cried. Kleenexes floated through the room. We were all reverent, ridiculously moved by Mr. Plummer's relief, by the vision of him walking, dazed, through the enormous house, by the sight of him standing barefoot on his private beach gazing out at the ocean, by the idea (imagine!) that he and his family might never again feel fear.

• • •

We began to make the calls telling the women of their reimbursements. A worker appeared on our floor, pushing a cart mysteriously filled with foods that we all liked; she came to the basement throughout the day, handing us chocolate chip cookies, potato chips, jelly beans; someone knew we needed to be nourished. We spent most of the day shut in our offices. Sometimes I walked to the water fountain and I checked to see what the others were doing. I saw Kayla splayed on the floor between calls, eyes closed, her arms stretched out, palms grasping the carpet; she had told me that she couldn't sleep. Jana asked for a punching bag for her office, and I saw her, between calls, lunge toward it again and again. Marianne had drawn the blinds on her office and through her door, I heard a soft sound that might have been weeping. The mail person dumped file after file on our desks.

Before each call, I ate one candy. The sweetness in my mouth was supposed to prepare me. I tried to conjure whatever in my voice I had been hired for: "We are delighted to offer you this reimbursement," but I did not know how to respond when they answered:

"That's it?"

"You're kidding, miss, right?"

"Is this an amount I will get weekly?"

"You fuckers. I still have to work here. No. No."

At the end of the day, we stood by the elevator, quiet now. Jana was looking increasingly fit from her bouts with the punching bag. My clothes were getting tight from my extensive consumption of chocolate. Despite her attempts at napping, Kayla looked like she had not slept in a year. Marianne's face was discolored when she reached the elevator, her eyes swollen; she had been crying most of the day.

We did not discuss our work. However, we did notice that our salaries were rising. The first week, by a hundred dollars. The second week, by two hundred. We brought this up, casually, with each other. The third week was different.

"Three hundred," said Kayla.

"I got one twenty-five," said Jana.

"Three seventy-five," I said.

"Mine didn't go up at all," said Marianne.

"What's going on?" said Kayla.

Waiting for the elevator, we were now alert in a new way. This information gave us a focus, something else to talk about. Why did each of us receive a different raise? We could not quit; no one ever quit anything ever, because, of course, there was nowhere to go; now, every Friday, when we received our paychecks, we met at the elevator and whispered our salary increases to one another:

One hundred dollars.

Seventy-five dollars.

Four hundred dollars.

We received our paychecks at four p.m. each Friday, and I tore open my envelope, my heart ablaze, to see what I got that week; by five p.m. we gathered by the elevator, telling each other what we had received. We revealed that week's salary with a beautifully calculated casualness, Kayla twisting her hair, Jana reaching her arms back in a stretch, none of us looking the other in the eye. We were not supposed to care, but our interest in these distinctions was a sort of spell. Now this was all we talked about.

When we began, I thought Marianne would be the worker least affected by the complaints and the meager reimbursements, but this was not the case. Marianne was looking worn out; she had cried about the complaints and reimbursements for some weeks but still worked through them with surprising and deliberate speed. I was tired myself, but I said I would take some of her files.

This is how I came to open Packet 3784. Her name was Joanne. She was from Southern California. She was my age, twenty-three, and she named the company where she worked. It was an advertising firm I had heard of, and she was a junior executive there.

She had an idea for an advertising campaign to promote a citrus soft drink, a good idea, and a guy working with her stole it. He saw it on her computer screen and took a screenshot and sent it to her boss. He received a bonus, five thousand dollars. She went to his office to insist on credit for her idea.

He started to beg; apparently he needed the bonus for his kid's medical bills. He almost wept but then his tone changed and he locked the door.

I read on.

• • •

After I read the packet, I had to get out of my office. My chest felt constricted, and the room suddenly seemed very small. I walked over to the water fountain past Kayla and Marianne and Jana, all of them at their desks and speaking into their phones with their kind voices. It was the sound I had become accustomed to each day, almost like a stream of running water, but suddenly the rush of their voices sounded like a language I did not understand. This frightened me. I remembered how excited I was to get this job, and looking down the dark hallway, I understood, with a sharp iciness in my heart, the finite quality of our lives, and that this would be the only job I would ever hold. For the first time, I wondered if I could do it.

I did not want to see what Joanne would ask for. I read further through the packet. The line where she was supposed to indicate an estimated reimbursement was blank. This was odd, and I didn't know how she could send in her complaint without that number; I imagined she was so distraught she had forgotten to include this. I thought of consulting Mr. Watson, but then remembered this was actually Marianne's packet, so I did not. I decided to call Joanne myself.

I dawdled for a couple of days, calling instead those with other reimbursements, speaking with a couple workers who thanked me (sincerely) for their thirty-four dollars and sixty-two dollars and asked me to please send on our list of recommended regional restaurants, which I did (lower price range).

Finally, I called her. My script sat in front of me.

"Yes," a voice said, very quietly.

"May I speak to Joanne Trotman," I said, warmly.

A long, stretchy silence. "Who is this?"

"My name is Miss Windham," I said. "I am calling from the Department of Workplace Grievances. We are glad you have submitted your claim to us. This is a preliminary call to check in. I wanted to see how you are doing."

She said nothing for a long moment.

"Hello?" I asked.

"Why are you calling," she asked, softly.

"I am calling because our great nation values your contribution to our workforce," I said, following the script. My voice, to me, sounded surprisingly loud.

"Our workforce," she said. "Is that what you call it."

The script did not indicate how I should answer a comment like this.

"I am speaking with Ms. Trotman?" I said.

"Of course you are," she said.

I decided to continue. "I am calling also because you left line forty-three, your request for reimbursement, blank on our official form," I said. "We cannot yet provide an exact estimate of what we can obtain for you, but we can assure you that your claim will be—"

There was a sound coming from her end of the line. A sharp honking, a knife slicing the air—no. A laugh. She was laughing, but not the kind of laughter I was invited to join; it was laughter that had the swooping cadence of crying, and I had the uncomfortable sense that she was laughing at me.

"Miss Trotman," I asked, "are you okay?"

"Okay," she whispered, fiercely. "Okay!"

"Are you?" I asked.

"Sometimes I feel like my office is full of bombs," she said. "There is one behind the potted palm. There is one in the stall in the women's restroom. There is one by the coffee machine. If they ever go off, the whole office will burst into flames and everyone's bones will melt as they run for the door—"

"Miss Trotman," I said, "I have to put something on line forty-three of your claim. To send it to our appraisal department—"

"The explosion would engulf him," she said. "He would be gone in an instant. That would be my reimbursement." She paused and sounded almost wistful when she said, "Can you do that for me?"

I put down my pen. My tongue felt numb. I stared at the script, the words arranged there; they did not resemble letters, but weird, contorted bars.

"At first, I woke up, got dressed, went to work," she whispered, in an even tone. "I did. I timed my entrance so that I would not see him. I did the same for lunch. I called in sick if we had a meeting together. But then I remembered. This is my job. I will be here forever, always listening for him—"

"Miss Trotman," I whispered. "Can you please give me a number—"

"That's not what I want," she said, terse. "I want you to do something else." She hung up.

• • •

My office was silent; for a while, I sat in that silence. I tried calling her back, once, twice, and then later that day. She didn't answer. The phone rang and rang; there was no machine to take a message. Even if she had picked up, though, I didn't know what I would say. I could not bear to ask her again to give me a number for her reimbursement. Line 43 was still empty, which meant I was useless in helping her.

At the end of the day, I stood up, walked out of my office, and saw my coworkers standing by the elevator. They looked tired, but not prohibitively so. Each one held a large bouquet of roses; they looked as though they had all placed in a beauty pageant.

"What happened?" I asked.

"Floor six left these for us," said Marianne. "By your mailbox."

I glanced over at our mailboxes, set by the elevator; inside mine was a large bouquet of roses, red and pale orange, the flowers surrounded by baby's breath. The bouquets smelled wonderful, and the air around us glimmered, sweet and pink.

"Are we being fired?" I asked, concerned.

"No, we all got cards," said Kayla, shrugging. The card said, *Thank you for your continued generosity and service.* In the elevator, we clutched the bouquets, wrapped in crisp white paper, and when we walked out into the dying light of the afternoon, I noticed how people glanced at us—with a sort of amusement, these women with bouquets, perhaps the recipient of love and flirtation—or with bitterness, unsure if we had received a promotion at work. The second interpretation was the most troubling for the observers. Kayla pressed her bouquet to her chest like a baby; Jana gripped hers like a torch.

Kayla slowed down to giggle, a little wildly. "I'm so glad my sweetie knew I liked roses!" she said a little too loudly, wanting others to hear her.

I understood. The bouquets had to seem romantic, or others might follow us. Gripping her bouquet, she rushed off.

I did not go home just then. Joanne's address was written on a scrap of paper in my pocket. I boarded a train that was not my train, toward a different neighborhood, about thirty minutes away. The roses, in their paper wrapping, made my palms cold and wet.

At her street, I got off and walked around. Her apartment was located at 37 West Street. She was in Apartment 6-A. It was an older building, the type guarded by regal, bored marble lions. I went to the entrance, scanned the mailboxes, found 6-A, and pressed the buzzer. It made a bleating sound. I waited and then pressed it again, for a longer moment. I waited. Then there was her voice. Soft but angry, like a sharp, digging knife.

"Who is this?"

I didn't answer.

"Hello?"

She hung up. I pressed the buzzer again.

"Hello! Who is this? Speak!"

I stood, frozen, as I didn't know what to say.

She hung up.

I paused, pressed the buzzer again, and then left my bouquet on the floor, right under her mailbox, and crossed the street. I didn't want to leave just then; I pretended I was looking for something on the sidewalk when I saw a woman step out of the building. I remembered her photo from the file, so I knew it was Joanne: late twenties, tall, very dark hair. She picked up the bouquet but regarded it with suspicion; her face was tight with fear. She looked up and down the street and I pretended I was brushing dirt off the leaf of a bush. I couldn't quite see her face, but her movements were quick, tense, as though she sensed some disturbance in the air. She tossed the bouquet into the street and went inside.

I waited there, as though I were now watching over her even if she did not know it, and I felt a readiness inside me, for an action, I did not know what—a desire to beat something back. I wanted to have a use. Or I wanted a different one than I already had, one that I could not articulate, that was what I wanted to tell myself—I wanted to turn myself inside out, be something new. I was just standing across the street like an idiot, watching for a threat I couldn't see.

After half an hour or so, I went home.

The next day, in the basement, the others continued to work on their packets, as usual, but with more energy; the bouquets seemed, oddly, to have cheered them. And a few days later, they gathered at the elevator, now compelled by another small item: everyone had received jars of imported jam in a basket. Rasp-

berry, blueberry, and apricot. The jars were tiny and adorable.
The basket was accompanied by another card. Our efficiency
was being rewarded. We were still receiving unequal raises,
but this, it seemed, led to another route of discussion—what
crackers or bread went best with the jams, who might bring
crackers in the next day, who preferred raspberry to peach,
and so forth.

I felt forced to display the basket in my office, but when
I opened the jam, the sweetness of the smell almost made me
choke.

My packets were going more slowly, jam and bouquets
notwithstanding. I kept looking back at Joanne's file, reread-
ing it as though hoping what was inside might change, that
what had happened did not happen, or not as I remembered
it. But each time I read her account, everything happened the
same way. I hoped I would see the story shift at key moments,
and sometimes felt sad to the point of tears or then angry
so that I felt hot light flash in my skin, or was other times
irritated, wishing that she had just unlocked the door and escaped. I tried to calculate an enormous, impossible reimbursement for her.

I went to Mr. Watson with Joanne's file to ask what to do
about line 43. I had forgotten that this was originally Marianne's file, but I noticed him glance at her name on the folder;
he froze.

"There has been some sort of mix-up," he said.

"Oh," I said, remembering. "I can be effective with all
files," I said.

He closed the file and pressed his hands flat against it. "I'll take this one," he said.

"I already spoke to her," I said. "I'd like to finish—"

"That's fine," he said, cheerfully, as though I had said something clse.

"I have time," I said, my voice more insistent. "I can—"

"It's no problem at all," he said. "Don't worry. By the way, did you like the jam? Which was your favorite?"

The file was right there, under his hand, and I wanted to lunge across the desk and grab it. But I didn't.

"Apricot," I said. When I returned to the basement, I passed the others, who were sitting in the pale glow of the TV in Marianne's office, watching *Your New Home*. In this episode, a man became so excited that he knew the answer to the question "What is the capital of Nebraska?" He tried to slam the buzzer with such force his hand missed and it didn't go off. Rules were rules; his competitor won; he had to be carried off the stage by three security personnel as he screamed that he was, in fact, the rightful winner. Part of a set toppled over; there was a scuffle offstage. The show instantly switched to a montage of the most recent family to win a mansion, with shots of them enjoying a catered dinner at their newly furnished, sixtieth-floor penthouse in midtown Manhattan. The city glimmered outside the window like an enormous jewelry box. The serving staff tenderly set sculpted chocolate desserts with red raspberries on each plate. We watched as the triumphant family leaned back in their chairs and released a buoyant laughter.

• • •

The next day, the mail person dumped a load of new files on my desk, about twice as many as I usually received.

"What is this?" I asked.

But I knew. Walking by the other offices, I noticed that my coworkers were not receiving the same number of files that I did. It was not that I was more efficient; Mr. Watson was trying to keep me busy.

I received less taxing files, involving mostly bizarre comments, and I read through them carefully. My voice was as tender as it always was, but I heard a new sound in it: a pause, a slight hesitation. This alarmed me, and I imagined my reluctance was something else—an oncoming cold, or simply tiredness. I tried to correct this hesitation, but I felt it, a slowness, as I spoke.

I left work early and again I took the train toward Joanne's apartment. I didn't think about it, I just wanted to go; I wanted to talk to her, to ask her what she wanted, if not a reimbursement, then what? Why file a claim at all? Our great nation could do something for her, I had to believe this was true; there was a fluttering in me, a feeling of spreading, of some expansiveness I could not name. The golden evening air around me was very clear. I stood on the sidewalk outside her apartment again. I waited.

I stood there for maybe an hour. Then she walked out. She was moving very fast, trying to cut a hole into the air in front of her. She was as sharp as scissors. I watched her walk down the street, and I wasn't sure how to proceed, but I found myself following her.

She turned a corner; I continued, about a half a block behind. She was striding along quickly, but then she glanced back and noticed me.

I had never followed anyone before, so I just continued. She rushed ahead, faster. I planned in my head what I would say to her, wanting to find the right words that would encourage her to name a reimbursement. Joanne turned a corner and she kept looking back; she went down a street and then I realized that she had made a circle and was approaching her building again.

She stopped.

Her hands were on her hips and her face was sharp with fear.

"Don't follow me," she said.

The street was empty, darkening. She stared at me as though I might hurt her, and I felt sadly misunderstood.

"Hello," I said, holding out my hand. "Miss Windham. I'm from the Department of Reimbursement."

She did not shake my hand.

"Why are you here?" she asked.

I shivered. "I am a representative from the Department of Workplace Grievances. You sent a complaint to us. We are here to help."

She stepped forward, just slightly. "You want to help? This is how you can help," she said. "Get rid of him. Get him fired. I want to walk through that office knowing that I never have to see him again in my life. I want him to vanish."

Her words lit up the street. How clear they were. I shivered, a little awed, listening to her.

"I see," I said, carefully.

"So do it," she said. She waited. She was like a giant sword standing there. She held some hope. I wanted to say anything but what I would say, I wanted to say yes, yes, we would do that, we would protect her. But I could not.

"We are unable to get involved in personnel issues," I said. "But we can offer you some money." My voice rose, tarnished. A shudder passed over her face. She stepped toward me and I thought she might shake my hand, finally, we would figure this out, and I was smiling, when she raised her hand and then whooom, her fist crashed into my face, and I crumpled forward, a streak of pain blazing through my head, and then Joanne was gone, and I was sitting on the sidewalk.

A woman rushed up to me. "Dear! Are you okay?" She held out a tissue and I pressed it to my nose, which was bleeding. The world was a little bent and hazy. She helped me stand.

"I think so," I said.

"You poor thing," she said. "Do you want to go to the ER?"

I sat on a bench and took some deep breaths. My nose slowly stopped bleeding; there was just a dull throb in my head. I was not a violent person, and I would not advocate violence toward others, and this was not the reaction that I expected from her. But I also had a thought that I did not want to admit; there was something about the pain in my head that felt somehow terribly logical and correct.

• • •

At the office, the others came over and inquired about my bruise, but I could not tell anyone what had happened. I had gone to the home of a person sending in a complaint, which I was not supposed to do. I touched my bruise with my fingers and I felt my conversation with Miss Trotman was not finished. This feeling of incompletion made me restless. I closed my office door and looked through that day's files, but I found that I could not concentrate on them; without Joanne's file to focus on, I was lost. I felt like I had a terrible itch on my scalp that I could not quite locate. After some pointless organizing and alphabetizing, I went to see Mr. Watson.

"I wanted to check on something," I said. "The file you took over. Were you able to figure out a reimbursement?"

"Which file?" he asked.

"Joanne Trotman," I said.

He nodded and gazed over my shoulder.

"Who?" he asked.

"Joanne Trotman," I said. "We discussed her case—"

He brushed his hand through the air, waving away some dust. "I don't know what you're talking about," he said.

"Joanne Trotman," I said, my voice rising just a little, and, in my mind, I felt a bright tinsel of fear. I leaned forward and my fingers gripped the edge of his desk.

"Please remove your hands from my desk, Miss Windham," he said, his voice cold. I lifted my hands. The discussion was over. A shriek built inside me but I could not let it out. There was a silence between us as thick and voluminous as a boulder. Mr. Watson scooted back his chair. He pushed a glass bowl of mints toward me.

"Would you like a mint?" he asked.

I shook my head no.

"Are you okay?" he asked, and I realized he was talking about my bruise.

"I had a little accident," I said. "I am fine."

He gave me a long, sad look.

"Good," he said. "You know our great nation needs you. You know how fortunate you are." He paused. "Maybe you can tell me, Miss Windham . . . why would anyone reject any opportunity? Why would anyone turn down what we have to give? Why would anyone not want to be part of this great country?" He leaned forward abruptly, as though blown toward his desk, and his face was pale and thin. "Or perhaps what I am saying is, why would anyone choose to separate from the rest of us? Why would anyone choose to be alone?"

Two weeks later, I went back to her apartment. Joanne's name was not listed on the mailboxes. I stepped outside and examined the building, wondering if I had the wrong address; but this was where she lived. When a man opened the door, a little dog eagerly pulling on a leash, I asked, "Have you seen Joanne Trotman? I thought she lived here."

The man stopped, his dog softly murmuring around our feet. "Who?" he asked.

"Joanne Trotman." I said her name, slowly.

"Dark hair, young? She in 6-A?"

"Yes," I said.

"No one lives there now," he said.

"What," I said.

"It's empty."

I felt myself breathe. Then I crouched, petted the dog, and asked, quietly, "Where'd she go?"

"I think she lived there until two weeks ago. Then I don't know, I heard some noise in her apartment one night, I think it was 6-A, and then I didn't see her anymore. No one knows where she went."

"What do you mean no one knows where she went?"

He shrugged. "She's gone. Management just dumped all her stuff on the sidewalk. You need anything? You can just take it. It's there."

I turned to look at the curb, where there was indeed a jumble of furniture; a blue couch, some lamps sitting on a dresser, a dining room table, a couple bookshelves, plates and towels and cups in cardboard boxes.

"Some of the lamps are rather nice," said the man; the dog strained at the leash, and they rushed off.

I looked at the furniture, everything that Joanne had owned, and I carefully settled myself on the blue couch. It had rained earlier that day, the fabric held the damp, cold scent of it. I sat on the couch where Joanne had been, and I wondered what she thought about everything before she started her job, if she had been happy to find it, what she hoped for when she started, what she arranged on her desk, and what her plans had been. I felt a chill against my skin but I did not move. I wished the couch would tell me where she was, but it did not. "Where," I said, out loud, but my voice did not help; I wanted to help. Day was sliding darkly into night, and I watched everyone coming home from work, or those who worked and those who pretended to, and I wondered where Joanne was now, and I wondered who I was, and about my place in this world; I knew that this would be my only job, in my one life, and that stacks of files were waiting on my desk at this very moment, and that there was, truly, nothing I could say to any of them. I sat there for a long time. The faces of the others, rushing by, blank, revealed nothing. A woman picked up one of Joanne's lamps, examined it, tucked it under her arm, and walked away. The damp couch sunk a little under the weight of my body. I wondered what would happen to all of us.

On a Scale of
One to Ten

Let's get this straight: We did not want to be here. We were Jews, and we were sitting in the principal's office of the missionary evangelical school. We were three people, two adults and our child. But we had decided to visit this evangelical school of our own free will. Not because we were religious, no. We were here because of the world's paucity of love.

Our history of religious belief was short and shoddy. Sometimes we went to temple, sometimes we tried to pray about various things, or joined the local Jewish group to feed the homeless.

We lived our lives in a midsized city in the American South, me, my husband, our daughter, age thirteen. We went to our places of employment, purchased groceries, bought new appliances when the old ones finally went bust, tried various diets, helped our daughter with homework, cheered at various competitive sports events, hoped for a raise, assembled salads for school and temple potlucks. At night, my husband's breath was hot on my ear. The sun rose and plunged behind acres of parking lots.

How did one gauge the invisible disturbances in others' feelings toward you? We went about our days. We liked some people while others annoyed us; they sometimes liked us and sometimes did not. My workplace was a shimmering combination of Americans, a semi-motley group, mostly Christian, a couple other Jews, a couple atheists, all of us trying to get ahead, but trying (mostly) to be polite about it, standing in line at the coffeemaker, placing little candies on desks during the holidays, etc.

My husband and I walked beside each other under a hard blue sky, trying to go forward, listening to the lovely, soft scrape of our feet against the ground.

Then, one evening after work, I was walking through the parking lot of our office. It was seven p.m. and the lot was an empty plain of dusky light. I was working with my new assistant, Jane, who had been with the company for just a month. It was her first job, and she, the niece of the president of the company, won it over seventy-two other candidates. We were all expected to welcome her. Her personality was as sweet as a plum. She had glossy hair that she wore styled up, like the wife of an astronaut. She was a little slow to finish her work. Earlier today, I had told her to rewrite part of a report. I said this in the most polite way one could when she had left out several important (and essential) facts, but she looked at me and blinked quickly, as though night had descended and I had suddenly become difficult to see.

I strode across the parking lot. Jane was sitting in her car. Suddenly, she backed out and started driving, her Prius heading fast, the wheels screaming. I stood, for a moment, watching the car come toward me. I thought, casually, that she should turn the wheel of the car. The headlights gave off a starry haze. A weirdly legalistic thought lodged in my head: as the pedestrian, I had the right-of-way. But then the car sped up, with a guttural sound, and I jumped out of the way.

Jane drove on, yelling "Move!" out the window. I was sprawled on the ground, breathing hard, like an animal, as though my breath understood something that I did not. My heart was a war. My hands peeled off the asphalt, skin crackling, my palms scraped with blood and gravel. Jane zoomed off to other activities.

What had happened, what?

I got into my car and it tumbled down the dark streets. There was even a little blood on the steering wheel, when I parked the car and released my hand.

I got home and saw that the trash cans were still on the curb. I brought them in and then I informed my husband what had happened.

"She did what?"

"She tried to run me down. In her Prius. Then she drove off."

I held out my hands, pink and scraped. He brought a damp towel over and cleaned them, very gently. He was shocked.

"Were there witnesses?"

"No."

"Security cameras?"

"No."

I was still confused; had this happened? It was so sudden and unexpected. That was the thing about violence—you never had time to prepare. You only thought of a good response much later. Did she really want to hit me? Or had she, perhaps, just wanted to get home? I wanted to make excuses for her, for the situation. Plus, there was that report she was supposed to correct. What would her response be if I made another helpful criticism? A grenade?

We stood in a dimly lit cage of confusion and fear.

"Did this really happen?" he asked.

I was affronted by his question; he didn't believe me. Then again, neither did I. It was so much simpler to believe that nothing happened. I wanted to believe in the boring moment before she drove toward me, the moment I was just walking across the parking lot, the moment I was just heading to my car to go home.

We lay in bed. The floor remained still, as always, as the earth whizzed, on its stubborn, lonely track, through the air.

• • •

First thing the next day, I marched upstairs and told my supervisor, who flinched and sent me up to Floor Eight. I told the person on Floor Eight that Jane had tried to run me down in her Prius. But my voice trembled, for even I did not quite believe it. She was the president's niece. She had that title. And no one had seen this but me.

Jane came into work, seeming refreshed by her night's sleep, wearing a crisp new blouse with, bizarrely, a bow. She was friendly to all, even me. I watched her carefully at work. It was as though nothing happened. The friendliness filled me with doubt. Had this happened in my dreams? But my palms were all I had to show, still raw from the parking lot. "Tell us if it happens again," the vice president said.

I was forty-seven, which meant sometimes I wanted to roll the world up like a ball and crush it. By this age, I had seen enough friends and family die, crumple, ascend, change political parties, decorate their homes so horribly you thought they had gone insane. There was the general sense that things were as sturdy as a piece of wet paper. But this was new. I had trouble concentrating. I did not want to walk by myself to the parking lot, which put me in a bad mood. And then there were the strange calls to our house.

"Run," the voice said. "Run."

Who was saying this?

Click.

Was this a threat? Who was telling us to run?

The next time, I shouted into the phone. "Who are you? Why are you saying this?"

"You know what to do."

It was Jane, maybe talking through a scarf.

"I'm telling your uncle!" I said. "Stop!"

My husband and I walked around, afraid. We told the police. They said walk more quickly across the parking lot. This was their advice? If there was no evidence, they sighed, there was nothing they could do. Jane was chatty as could be in the office; she told funny stories about her Chihuahua and everyone laughed. Sunlight poured through the office windows.

The office park remained encased in its veneer of normalcy, but the difference between what one saw and what one knew made the world appear warped, perceived through a glass paperweight. It made me afraid.

Fear did not make one a more noble or understanding person. My husband and I began to find fault with each other. Why didn't you take out the garbage? Why did you eat that blueberry yogurt? Why did you buy that Osterizer when you had two cavities filled last month? At night, I related what Jane had done that day, which was always puzzlingly ordinary. Sometimes, she had trouble using the stapler. She changed her fingernail polish from beige to gold. There was nothing to be learned from any of this. Streetlights turned yellow to red, planes blew across the sky, strangers in dark corners kissed or lunged at one another with knives.

We clutched each other at night, arms wrapped tightly around the crinkly bags that were our bodies. We tried, softly, to climb into the dim, sweet recesses of each other. But we did not know if we could protect each other from the strange, violent tremors in the world.

Really, we just had to get out of there.

So I quit.

I looked for a new job. I looked and looked and looked and finally there was this. A company that took me on. Here, they said, here is a good salary. They wanted to ship us off to another nation, across the shining Pacific.

Okay, we thought. A new future! A gift.

But we had a daughter. One child. And she was concerned. What would it be like?

"I'll miss Donna's birthday," she said. "She's having a laser tag go-kart birthday!"

There was the soddenness of irreversible loss. But we had to say yes to this assignment. It was good money. It was a door. How could you not go through a door when it was offered?

"Say I'll be invited to birthdays," she said. "Promise."

"Promise," we said.

"Okay," she said, standing up straight, tucking her shirt in, "okay."

• • •

So this new job was just a job, in a growing city, in Asia. It was another continent—another language, different behavior at stoplights. But here, no one tried to run me down. We had an apartment at the top of a large granite building. We walked the streets, awash with color, by the huge malls, twelve floors of purses and jackets and shoes, the fierce neon of a small nation wanting people to notice it, bringing in companies, selling things, flying us here.

At first, all was well. Our daughter was excited, she tried squid on a stick, she learned to order bubble tea in Chinese. People on the bus gazed at her, called her *piaoliang*, beautiful. Coworkers took us to eat dumplings.

But there was a problem, how could we not know there would be a problem.

The students at the lauded international school were a group of hoodlums from around the world. Our daughter walked through the doors of this beautiful international academy and global harmony went to hell. The daughters of business moguls from China, Thailand, India, Korea, England, Italy, Lebanon, Germany, Russia, Australia. Even Las Vegas. At first, gestures of alliance. A loaned bottle of nail polish. A meet-up at the mall. Then, a general revolt across all countries. It was not clear what went wrong.

Our daughter said she couldn't find the girls in her class during lunch. They sat in class, hair pulled back in ponytails, well behaved, crisply taking notes. What could go wrong? At lunch, at recess, they vanished. Every damn country in her grade. Even Las Vegas.

Where were they?

They weren't telling her.

Someone, on a regular basis, started stealing her lunch. It vanished, the remains left on the cafeteria table. Empty wrappers. They ate everything. She came home sad and starving.

We had numerous stern, unproductive conferences with the headmaster of the school.

"Do something," we said to the headmaster. "Can't you do something? Stop this."

He proved himself incapable of controlling any nation in the world. Our daughter kept her lunch zipped up in her backpack all day, reaching inside to make sure it was there. Sometimes it was, sometimes she left her desk for a moment and it was not.

We sat around the table at night, our daughter hungry, head in her hands.

So this was what happened to our new start. We gripped the edges of the kitchen table as though it would tip and throw us overboard at any moment. Our daughter sobbed. I never prayed, I was not that type, the night swelling, dark, outside the windows. It seemed we had missed some lesson, or perhaps just had a bout of bad luck, but there was the terrible sense that our hands were useless. They dangled at the ends of our arms. We could not bend the world to anything we wanted. I looked into the night sky, and thought, *How do we help her? Or ourselves, Adonai? What do we do?*

So *Adonai*, or someone (actually me), said, let's see if we can find another school. And this evangelical school was the only other school that taught in English and had a spot open.

So here we were, walking into the Jesus school, across the shining, well-trimmed, extremely clean campus. We were lost, in a way; we did not know what we would find. Our fear kept us separate; we did not hold hands. Our daughter walked in front of us, looking at everything with hopeful interest. We walked in our clothes that we hoped would convince them. Not our best shoes. My husband in a slightly worn jacket. We had done this as a strategic measure. It looked a little as though we had blown here, pieces of trash off the surface of the world.

The principal was named Mr. Adams. He was tall and bald and his face looked like it had been molded out of pink clay. His lips were large and lush and somehow beautiful. His eyes were bright. It was a steady, unnerving brightness, as though he had a furnace inside his head.

"Sit however you want," he said.

There were two couches. Was this a test? How should we sit? What would he learn about us from our choices? We need to make a good impression on him, on Jesus, on whoever decided admissions. We decided to sit beside each other, to approximate a unified front.

"Nice school," I said. "Great facilities—"

"Thank you," he said.

He looked at me, those eyes blazing.

"Why are you here?" he asked our daughter.

"I'm here because kids at the other school steal my lunch," she said.

We are here, I wanted to say, because we failed. Because here was the child, the dear one we were entrusted to protect.

"What are your favorite subjects?" the principal asked our daughter.

"Latin."

Latin! Smart answer. Was this strategic?

"Anything else?"

"I like math," she said.

The principal sat forward as though someone had kicked him.

"You know this is a Christian school," he said.

We all startled, as though surprised by this, though, of course, it was true.

"What do you think about that?" he asked.

What were we supposed to say? We wanted him to save us, but not in the way he was thinking. We sat, aggressively having no thoughts, or not the ones that were perhaps required.

We were here because we wanted something small but essential. A community that would be nice to our child, to us. But the truth was that we, as Jews in a mostly Christian city, had spent years telling people who invited us to church, no. No, we don't believe in Jesus. He was a nice man, that's it. *Shema yisrael adonai elohaynu*, blah, blah. One god, they're all the same. Repair the world, help the poor, the victims of genocide, don't let the Holocaust happen again. No forcing anyone to believe what you do. That basically summed up our theology. We had relatives who had fled pogroms, concentration camps; we had the candelabra passed down from a tenement in Brooklyn to a suburb in Ohio. We had read some of the Torah, sort of; we could stumble through a few prayers. But we felt we were Jews in some basic way; we knew we were not something else.

"Uh, nothing," our daughter said. "There's a cross in the front." She paused. "It's really big."

We heard how she said that, really big, as though she found that perplexing.

The principal took a breath.

"I know that the cross might seem strange to people," he said. "What happened there. But to us the cross is a beautiful and endearing symbol."

His eyes got brighter; they were almost teary.

"What our school and our teachers want to share is their relationship with Christ," he said. "Not what kind of Christmas tree you have, or baptism, or what have you, but our deep relationship with God, which we want to share. Head, heart, hands."

He tapped his head, heart, and held out his hands. He said this in deep, kind tones. He was in love, it was clear. He actually glowed with it. And he wanted to share it. How nice that seemed! How generous!

The room felt close, stuffy, full of this invisible love. I had just wanted a safer school for our daughter, some friends she could sit with, and a lunch that no one would steal; I had not expected this offer. It was suddenly a little hard to breathe. It felt like a million Jesuses were surrounding me, pressing against me. I sat up and took a deep breath from the bottom of my lungs.

My husband sat beside me, and I was frustrated by our grubby humanness, the way neither he nor I had been able to fix things, the situation with Jane or now this with the lunches. The world cleverly slipped through whatever walls we nailed up.

Last night, my husband and I had had sex the way you do when you feel you have been idiots, wondering how we had found ourselves in this new nation, what we had done wrong. But we had grabbed arms and legs as though trying to break each other apart, to find some bigger clarity better than both of us. The Jesus of sex. Was that our Jesus? What did the principal mean? Did he ever think of Jesus when he had sex and was that weird or considered correct?

"What do you mean?" I asked the principal.

"You can't explain it," he said. "The teachers just share what they have felt. Jesus has meant so much to me. He has helped me, he is there for me always, he fills me up."

I envied his certainty, but was also wary of it.

"So," he said, looking at us. "We've heard you are—Jewish?"

This was true.

"On a scale of one to ten, what kind of Jew are you?"

Silence. He asked this with a kind of sweet curiosity.

"That's a hard question," said my husband.

The principal leaned forward. "Why?"

"I don't know any prayers," he said.

I didn't know so many either. This was just sad. God wasn't even mentioned. We had few thoughts on God, to be honest. We did eat matzoh on Passover, that was one thing. Though we also sometimes cheated with bread. Our faith was perhaps hard to describe, but we knew that it was not this other thing.

"Sometimes when I stand up with everyone and hear the music," I said, "I feel a little weepy."

The principal perked up, as though he knew me. Weepy, a bond. We both loved that bigger, generous idea of love, that was true. A great hand that we could all just step into, which could wipe away anything else. What did this mean for the principal and me? Did we love each other, maybe? It felt like there were too many people in the room, the three of us, Jesus, and what have you. It was too much love, too confusing. Wasn't his wife jealous of this extra person? I shivered.

It was wonderful to be loved. Who could argue with that? Who wouldn't want a large hand to hold you when someone tried to run you over in the employee parking lot or when you received strange calls in the night or when you wanted to throttle all the girls who stole your child's lunch?

I looked around and wondered: Why were we all so ridiculous? How did other people know how to be loved? How did they not almost get run over by someone in the office or have their lunch stolen at school, how did they know what to say to each other when they were afraid, parent to child, husband to wife? Was there a word, whispered in the dark, which would calm us? Was it a word we didn't know and Jesus did?

Was this what he meant, this principal?

But.

"So, let's go take a look at the campus," he said. Our daughter was escorted by a smiling young woman, Ruth, off to classes. We would meet at the chapel in an hour. We walked around the campus. It was luxurious with sun. It was as though this brightness had been ordered from a catalogue. Everyone seemed to be in a good mood. We walked, the four of us—me, my husband, the principal, and the invisible one. Or two. What about Jesus's father, then? Where was he in all of this? How many divine figures walked with us, loving us or not loving us, helping us or abandoning us?

The principal regarded me. He appeared to be full of love, but a love that got a little ragged by the middle of the afternoon. He checked his watch.

"How did you get into this line of work?" I asked the principal.

"My parents," he said. "I was a missionary kid. They took me to India, Kenya, Guatemala, I helped them build schools. My mother died when I was ten, my father and my sisters and I moved around, building houses for the poor, Jesus was there for me. He was there for me in the middle of the night, I felt him with me."

He stood beside us, a dark figure against the sun.

"You can peek in the classrooms. We will meet at the chapel in an hour."

He hurried off. We walked through the campus blanched with light. We peeked into a gym class, and the gym teacher was saying, "Run as fast as you can, run with these great bodies that God gave you!" and the math teacher was saying, "Jesus divided by what equals love?" and the art teacher was pinning up drawings of the Christmas star, the baby looking beatific beneath it.

We stood under the sky, a fragile blue tarp; beneath it, we felt almost invisible. Most people were invisible to other people, except when others saw them and wanted to harm them. The students rushed past us, going to their classes. I felt sorry for them and also envious, for their innocence, for their misunderstanding of what the world could be.

"How did we end up here?" my husband said, looking slightly haunted by the discussion in the math classroom.

How did anyone end up anywhere? I just wanted an answer. Worse, I had none. His brown hair was sticking up a little, and I smoothed it down. We huddled close together, though it did not feel cold outside. He put his hand on my shoulder.

"Will she choose Christ?" he asked, wondering.

I shuddered. What a thought. What would this mean? Everyone did seem content, perhaps scarily so. The teachers, the students, united, aglow. Maybe we were being unfair. This wasn't conversion through torture, beatings, etc. It was an offering through niceness, through a promise. The feeling of love, at first wanting to pull the person over you like a glove.

But.

An alarm sounded. The students poured out of the buildings into the main quad. We saw our daughter walking with a couple of kids, a boy and girl, chatting.

"She looks happy," said my husband.

Our daughter waved to us and then ignored us.

The bells chimed; it was time for chapel. If our daughter came here, she would have to come to the chapel each week. We went in and found a seat. We were here as witnesses, that was all. We wanted to feel a love that would protect us all. The students filed into an enormous auditorium. It was an assembly. Our daughter sat with members of her grade.

"Today we're not having our regular service," said the principal. "We have some personal testimonies by members of our school community."

There was a guitar, of course, and songs about Our Father. There was swaying. I noticed a few students texting, which made me love them.

Jason, a junior, stood onstage and talked about his upcoming surgery. He was going to have the scoliosis in his back corrected. He glowed in a yellow spotlight. "I was at the doctor's office and I found out all the risks of the surgery. I have to say, I was scared. Reading the risks, it said that I could possibly be paralyzed or die."

He was slight, and his voice cracked. His braces glinted in the light. His fear was a bright, cold ball in my heart.

"I was so scared, I didn't know what would happen. And then I felt Jesus's presence beside me. I was full of peace. I knew he was there for me." His voice swelled, rich, sonorous, as though he were in a play. It was a voice that trumpeted certainty, peace.

There was applause.

There was more singing. I felt a headache coming on, along the back of my neck, and a sharp, sudden cramp in my foot. I could barely stand. I put a hand on my husband's shoulder, and he looked at me, and I was surprised that there were tears in his eyes, too, and I was shaking out my foot, which felt like a club. I was being transformed into a freak for Jesus to heal, just by being around all this.

I had to get out.

I turned and limped out, pushing open the chapel doors, limped into the jabbing white light of the world. My husband and daughter were still inside. How long could they listen to this? What did they feel about this? What were they going to do?

I stood in the glare. It was so quiet out on the lawn, the machinery of cicadas, while inside there was singing.

I stood alone on the lawn, waiting for who would come out the doors. Would it be the principal? Jesus himself? It could be anyone. I felt like running, but from whom? To whom? There was no car zooming toward me this time; there were just the cicadas. I limped around. The arch of my foot was shot through with pain.

The doors opened; my husband walked out. Inside the chapel, the singing shuddered and rolled. I was standing by a tree, shaking out my foot.

He walked toward me and took my foot. He squeezed it, gently. "Harder," I said. He squeezed it more. The cramp began to subside. We looked at each other with relief; we were here, we knew each other, even if we didn't know how to maneuver around life, what was around us. We knew the unholy goldenness in our hearts.

My foot was better. I could stand on it now. And then, through the swarm of students leaving the chapel, came our child. Walking beside another girl. They laughed together. The other girl raised a hand, in a casual gesture of alliance, and vanished.

Our daughter rushed toward us, quickly, stepping so lightly across the lawn.

She nodded when she saw us, enough to just acknowledge us without being caught. We all walked, sort of together, from the crowd.

"What do you think?" I asked her, wondering what she had found here.

She kicked the grass a bit, watching the other kids.

"The kids are nice," she said. "But."

"But what?"

"Why were all the kids crying? I was standing there and everyone around me was crying."

"Maybe they're sad," I said.

With this reasoning—perhaps everyone was sad. We all walked together, the three of us, out the gates of the campus, back to the regular world, which awaited us, bubbling, lurking.

"There is that girl at the other school," she said. "She sat next to me once. Julie."

"Who's she?"

"From Singapore. She gave me some potato chips. And a piece of gum."

She dug into her pocket and brought out a couple of pieces of gum. Doublemint.

"You want some?"

She kindly handed us some gum. We all started chewing. We stood before her like disciples. We were, in fact, disciples of her, our child. We were disciples of each other, of our fingertips and eyelashes and hair, gazing at the long shadows we made under the hot glare of the sky.

We didn't know what would happen. We didn't know if Julie would be a friend or not. We didn't know who around us would be good. We walked out of the Jesus school, away from the principal, the nice kids, the love we were rejecting. It may have worked for them. It may have been their salvation. There were different realities, that's for sure. But we walked back toward our bruised, strange world instead, the three of us, away from Jesus's desire to love us. We had this instead, each other, our raw diamond-like somethingness. The air was warm above our scalps. We could smell our minty breath, hear the scrape of our shoes against the gravel parking lot. I walked with them, listening to us.

The Cell Phones

The rabbi told us, as he always did, to turn off our cell phones before he began the service. So I pressed that button on the side of the phone and saw its long face go dark. I was ready to reform, after all. It was, again, Rosh Hashanah. It was the beginning of the New Year, which meant that it was time to contemplate my various failings and imagine how to become a better person. I stood at the cusp of the year, surrounded by other members of Beth-Em Synagogue, everyone clad in their suits and fine dresses and pumps and satin yarmulkes. How elegant we all looked, how shimmery and crisp and presentable. The scents of rose and orange drifted through the air. It seemed that all of us had taken special care dressing this year. We were shoulder to shoulder, we knew each other and we didn't, and inside, everyone was grimy in a precise, individual way.

We all peered into the ark, its tall oak doors now open. The sheer white curtains floated lightly over the Torahs, adorned in their crimson velvet cases; they looked as though they were ready to go to an expensive restaurant or a wedding. The cantor's voice soared as he sung the deep notes of "Avinu Malkeinu," all of us bowing slightly before the ark, trying to appear humble, or concerned, assuming the blank and philosophical expressions particular to the High Holy Days. The other congregants were so focused I envied them. There was the temple secretary, Chaya Weiss, skilled at silence while voices argued over her; her eyes were closed and her eyelid twitched as she, perhaps, viewed her transgressions, whatever they were. There was Max Lowenstein, ten years old and wriggly; he was still for a moment, chin lifted, hands by his sides, as though at a military parade. And there was Gina Gordon, twelve, standing very straight in three-inch heels, glancing, with veiled interest, at everyone from her new height. Everyone appeared to be closer to imagining their better selves. I was trying, too, to imagine this, but my mind kept swerving the wrong way.

I considered the catalogue of my personal failures. There was the time I snapped at the cashier at the supermarket when she refused to give me a student discount even though

I was not a student; there was the fact that I never returned the cashmere sweater that Mara Stein loaned me because I found it soft and comforting in a way I could not release. There was the moment I swooped in and stole a parking place from Stan Tamkin, whose truck was adorned with the worst bumper stickers, and who was sitting, unfortunately, just a few rows away from me. There was the time I yelled at those who had done nothing really and were just in the way of my anger, and there were the many times I woke up, read the newspaper, and felt like a pancake of defeat. I closed my eyes and tried to see myself as different. I wished I could move through this bruised, shoddy world like a giant, in a way that was grand and brave and perhaps even helpful, but whenever I tried to imagine this version of myself, my mind slammed shut. I was a dwarf of bitterness. And I was not able to access this better self, no, for I was mired in my own personal grievances.

I wanted. I wanted everything I shouldn't; I wanted a load of cash and a Jacuzzi tub in our bathroom and everyone to stop yelling and I wanted everyone in this nation to shut up and listen to me. Why couldn't everyone just listen to me? I wanted sometimes to escape to another life and I wanted to freeze time so my children and husband would always be who they were at certain perfect moments and I wanted my family and friends to appreciate the love I wanted to lavish on them, but everyone kind of preferred their own sort of love, which was their choice, naturally, but it sometimes made me sad. I wanted my parents and an aunt and some friends who were dead to be alive again, and I could not get accustomed to, and even bitterly resented, their deadness. I wanted my brother to stop being mad because I had taken the best chandelier out of our parents' dining room. I wanted the cats to stop napping and clean up the house. I wanted to eat ten Entenmann's coffee cakes and not gain a pound. I wanted to climb back into my mother and try again to be born. I wanted to go completely deaf when some people were talking, and I wanted others to simply vanish. I wanted to ram my car into the minivan of Angela Price, whose son bullied mine.

I wanted, how I wanted to grab hold of and repair my broken nation, before it slipped away and vanished.

I looked at the congregants standing around me. They all gazed at the ark, faces slowly starting to open. Everyone appeared to be reasonably alert. I did not know what any of them wanted from themselves, or from our nation. But I knew what I did.

I wanted a nation in which our leaders never lied and were elected to office because of their love for and adherence to the truth. I wanted a nation where, if people got sick, they would be cared for, swiftly, tenderly, and the only concern would be that they would get well. I wanted a nation that did not conjure suspicion about entire groups of people, and did not assault or kill them, a nation where everyone could look each other, kindly, in the eye and say hello. I wanted a nation that did not just roll around, naked and panting, in piles of money, and where people who held fistfuls of it were actually able to say, "Here! You have some, too." I wanted a nation that did not order those who wanted to be here to just get out, go away, and brutally cart them off, but instead welcomed them, and learned and kindly said all their names. I wanted a nation where women could stroll leisurely through dark parking lots, city streets, everywhere, and never look behind them because they would never have any fear. I wanted a nation where a person could go to school or shopping or wherever and never worry about whether it was smarter to dive under a chair or run. I wanted a nation where people did not view one another as zombies because they were not zombies, because they wanted the best not just for themselves but also for each other. I wanted a nation where people loved one another, even strangers, because they had that much feeling inside of them, because they were that alive.

I sort of wanted to repent but really I wanted others to repent. I wanted the whole damn world to repent, to stop behaving terribly, and just, for once, be good.

Then a cell phone started to ring.

It was a cheery, slightly irritating tune, the unmistakable melody of a device that wanted you to grab it and make it stop playing. I thought, what idiot left his cell phone on, and looked around, and then, I realized with a jab of horror that the melody was coming from somewhere around my feet.

The ringing phone was mine.

I grabbed my bag. How could my phone be on? I had turned it off. We were in the middle of services! I was not this dumb. My hands were shaking, and I fumbled with the phone, forgetting how to turn it off. The damn thing kept ringing.

My hands were as clumsy as enormous mitts, and somehow could not figure out how to silence the phone, so, instead, I answered it.

"Marry me," said a stranger's voice.

The members standing in the pew behind me glared. The cantor's voice soared, grand, through the room.

"Uh, wrong number," I whispered.

"Please. You know I'd be good," said the voice.

I was trembling. Everyone in the congregation knew the phone belonged to me. They were concentrating very intently on their holiness—oh the pure focus of their blank faces!— and I had interrupted them.

"Stop!" I said, and hung up. I pressed the button on the side, the Power button, so the phone would turn off and I could get back to my quest for a higher self.

The phone rang again.

What the hell? The phone was off. Seriously. Now the cantor was looking, none too happily, at me.

I answered it. "Yes?" I whispered.

"I'm calling about the job," said a woman, sounding nervous.

"There's no job," I hissed.

"But I need it!" she said. "Please! Give it to me! Now!"

I hung up.

I looked around. The activity by the ark had ceased. There was no pretense of worship anymore.

I shrank to a puddle of shame. Happy Rosh Hashanah from me, the idiot whose cell phone had gone off. Twice.

"Honey, don't you know how to turn your phone off?" asked Eva, whose husband died a year ago.

I held out the phone, as evidence. Eva's best friend, Harriett, who ran a catering business, sat beside her; skeptically, she eyed the phone.

"Apparently, she does not," Harriet murmured to Eva.

"It's off!" I said. "I swear!"

I could feel everyone staring at me. How had I been so thoughtless, so careless? Didn't I see how others were trying to better themselves? Why couldn't I? Did I want to? Or was I, perhaps, a saboteur of others' desire to improve?

Another phone rang.

But this time it wasn't mine. Thank all gods everywhere. Everyone looked around. Another tinny melody erupted across the room. A woman gasped and rummaged through her purse. She brought it out, the phone happily ringing away.

"It was off!" she cried. But she answered it. On speaker.

"I got a bad diagnosis," a man's voice said. "I've got to quit my job. And hire someone to take my place. But to hell with it! I won't—"

Another phone rang. Then another. The rabbi and cantor, the temple president, various high-ranking members stood bewildered, suddenly ineffectual in the presence of these spirited ring tones. All the phones were going off at once, and the entire congregation seemed to be scrambling through their purses and pockets, pulling out their phones and answering them.

My phone was ringing again, too. Each time I shut it off,

it burst into its fierce song. Each time it rang, a person wanted something. Urgently. Or they were going to act.

"If the elevator keeps breaking I'm suing the building. Now."

"If you tweet those photos of yourself I swear I will take your phone and smash it against the wall—"

"Stop," I kept saying, and snapping my phone off. Would they just shut up already? Who wanted to hear the world's complaints? The world was mad, as in disappointed, humiliated, hurt, resentful, confused, lost, and everyone had personal solutions to this, most of which were inadvisable. They were human, most solutions were inadvisable. All of the congregants were answering their phones and going pale. No one was listening to the calls but instead, everyone was annoyed and confused by the rush of the ring tones. But the calls kept coming, on and on, and the pleas became more high-pitched and urgent. The cell phones sang and bleeped and whirred and filled the sanctuary with an unholy ruckus, and no one knew what to do.

"Rabbi, how do we make it stop?"

The rabbi gazed, bewildered, upon all of us. He clearly didn't know. My phone rang again.

"My dog ran away," a woman said. "I don't want to leave the house."

I was about to hang up, but this time, the phone trembled, living, warm, in my hand. There was a feeling in her voice that I understood. A sadness. The most human sound in the world. I understood this more than any words. So I did not turn off the phone.

"I know," I said. "Sometimes, I feel the same way."

I waited. There was the sound of a human breathing.

"Thank you," said the voice, and hung up.

The phone shuddered in my palm. And then it was off. It seemed to be off. I almost wanted to call her and continue the discussion, but I did not.

Then I heard, very clearly, the voice inside the phone of Frieda Sonnenbaum, who was standing beside me. In her phone, a man said, "and for the last year George, my son, started drinking, and he won't talk to me. My son. I drove him across the whole state of North Carolina for his basketball games when he was a kid, and he was an honors student in college and he drove drunk to our house and we started meetings but I just want to drive to his apartment, grab the bottles of liquor, and empty them into the street . . ."

This man was upset. Of course he was, but I heard something else in his voice, too. I grabbed Frieda's phone. She was a real estate agent, and not one who relinquished her phone easily. But this time she did.

"It's hard," I said. "I know. It is."

There was silence.

"Yep," said the man, and hung up. Frieda stared at me. I gently placed the quiet phone in her hand.

The phones exploded into sound, over and over, in the room until this. Until the person who answered the phone did not tell the one on the other end to stop. The phones were adamant, ferocious for attention, their rings shrieking so that it felt as though they would reside forever in the air, but as soon as we said something to the person on the other end, anything but "stop," the phones ceased their ringing. One by one, the ringing vanished and after a few minutes, finally all the cell phones in the temple were silent.

The silence in the room seemed new, it seemed enormous. The congregation looked a bit shaken. My ears felt a bit tender from all the buzzing. I was depleted. But now, the air was pure as glass. In this silence, I felt I could hear everything. Or I could try, perhaps, to listen.

We stood in front of the rabbi, who gazed at all of us, pleased.

"We are all ready now?" he asked us.

We were. I think we were ready. There was so much that all of us needed to fix. The world was still hot and despairing and full of pain, and I wasn't a giant at all, but I wasn't dust, either. I was trying to be a hopeful resident of the world. I stood with my fellow congregants in the room, feeling their presence beside me. We were all paying attention now, our minds unfastened. We looked to the new year. Here it was.

"All right then," the rabbi said. "Let's begin."

Acknowledgments

As always, with special appreciation to the wondrous team at Counterpoint: to my essential, visionary editor Dan Smetanka, and the tireless publicist extraordinaire Megan Fishmann. To my agent, Maria Massie, for wonderful, nourishing support. With many thanks to Hollins University for giving me a place to write and teach, for that essential support. To Paula Whyman for creating *Scoundrel Time*, that artistic outlet that has been a comfort. To the following beloveds: David and Meri Bender; my sisters, Suzanne and Aimee; my cousins Natalie and Shelley; Frances Silverglate, Perrin Siegel, Sean Siegel, warriors for justice, all. To dearest Margaret Mittelbach, Jennie Litt, Tim Bush, Katherine Wessling, Amy Feldman, Dana Sachs, Jenny

Shaffer, Bill McGarvey, Eric Wilson, Malena Morling, David McGlynn, Peter Trachtenberg, Elizabeth Cohen, and Don Baker, for being there, and for reading, always. And with so much love to my dear partner in everything, Robert, who said, always, to keep going; and, with endless love and pride, to Jonah and Maia, who learned, quickly, how to march.

"The Cell Phone" was published in a different form as "The Cell Phone That Would Not Stop Ringing During High Holy Day Services" in *The Saranac Review*, Fall 2015. "The Good Mothers in the Parking Lot" originally appeared, in slightly different form, in *Scoundrel Time*.

KAREN E. BENDER is the author of *Refund*, a finalist for the National Book Award for fiction, short-listed for the Frank O'Connor International Short Story Award, and long-listed for the Story Prize. She is also the author of the novels *Like Normal People* and *A Town of Empty Rooms*. She has won grants from the Rona Jaffe Foundation and the NEA, and is fiction editor for the literary journal *Scoundrel Time*. She is the Visiting Distinguished Professor of Creative Writing at Hollins University, and lives in Virginia with her husband, the author Robert Anthony Siegel, and their family. Find out more at karenebender.com.